Heroes, Myths and Legends

Heroes, Myths and Legends

Alan Jamieson

Illustrations by Reginald Gray

Ward Lock Limited · London

© Alan Jamieson 1978
Illustrations © Ward Lock Limited 1978

First published in Great Britain in 1978
by Ward Lock Limited, 116 Baker Street,
London W1M 2BB, a member of the Pentos Group.

Layout by Steve Tate

Text filmset in 12 on 14pt 'Monophoto' Apollo
by Servis Filmsetting Limited, Manchester.

Printed and bound in Singapore by
Toppan Printing Company

British Library Cataloguing in Publication Data
Jamieson, Alan
  Heroes, myths and legends.
  1. Legends – Juvenile literature
  2. Mythology – Juvenile literature
  I. Title
  398.2'08   PZ8.1

ISBN 0-7063-5711-6

Contents

Introduction

Many of the famous stories of classical literature have their origin in myth and legend. From these days centuries ago myths and real events merge into fantasies and sagas about heroes and giants, monsters and maidens, magic powers and all kinds of dramatic and startling adventures. The voyages and the battles, in which courage and loyalty, trickery and deception are often mixed, have passed into popular story-telling. Some of these tales have led to long poems that tell of life and death, love and war, loyalty and treachery. We do not always know how far these stories are all myth and how far some of them may be rooted in history. People argue about whether or not there was a real Robin Hood or a King Arthur and if the first men to sail from Europe to North America were the Vikings of Leif Ericsson. The Indian chief Sitting Bull, El Cid and Roland were real enough, but their deeds have been magnified by centuries of story-telling so that these heroes of legend become larger than life. Many of the world's greatest stories belong to Greek legend: Odysseus is of the Greece of the Trojan War, and his adventures are told in the *Odyssey*. Of these stories the tale of the one-eyed giant, the Cyclops, has caught the imagination of generations of children. And Theseus, who conquered the terrifying Minotaur, and Jason, in his long search for the Golden Fleece, are also part of Greek legend. Rama, on the other hand, comes to us from Indian mythology. With Sita, his faithful wife, he is to be found in the epic poem the *Ramayana* (written about 300 BC), in painting and in sculpture. How Rama overcame the powerful demon Ravana is a story that thrills children in any continent. Siegfried emerges from the ballads and songs which in the thirteenth century were brought together by Austrian troubadours in the *Poem of the Nibelungen*. Many German poets went to the Siegfried legend for their inspiration, and Richard Wagner brought to Brunhilde and Siegfried the gift of his music. Cuchulain's exploits are part of Irish legend; Tristan has appeared in Wales, Cornwall and Brittany; Horatius belongs to the early days of Rome. Volund the Smith is a more gruesome tale and, like the Flying Dutchman and Black Colin of Loch Awe, he is one of the heroes who suffer for their deeds. These stories are full of exciting adventures, magic powers, giants, battles, the victory of good over evil. The colourful and dramatic pictures help to deepen children's imaginative involvement in the adventures, adding a different dimension to their enjoyment.

Odysseus and the Cyclops

Odysseus, King of the land of Ithaca, was on his way home. After a long war against the city of Troy, he and other Greek soldiers sailed for their homelands. Odysseus had twelve ships in his fleet, and they made a fine sight as they dipped and rose on the blue sea. But a storm blew up and carried the ships towards a strange island. Exhausted by their struggle with the wind, the men were glad to step on the beach and to rest there.

Next day the Greeks noticed the smoke of fires on the mainland not far away. They could hear goats and sheep bleating. The sound of men's deep voices carried to them over the sea. Odysseus decided to explore. He left most of his ships and men on the island and took only one ship. Loading it with bread and strong wine, the Greeks set off for the mainland. As they neared it, they could see a cave in the cliffs with a stone wall built outside its entrance. Warily they waded ashore and explored the cave. It was empty except for some young sheep and goats. Someone had built the wall to keep them imprisoned. Someone had left pails and bowls for milking. And someone had made cheeses that

were bigger than a man's height. Odysseus' men wanted to steal the cheeses and return to their ship. But Odysseus refused. He was curious. He wanted to see who lived there. It was so quiet and peaceful – there could be no danger from a shepherd.

He chose twelve men and sent the others back to the ship. The twelve men followed him into the cave. They were afraid, but Odysseus was their commander and they would obey him in all things. They waited and waited. No one came. They relaxed, lit a fire, toasted and ate some of the cheeses and fell asleep. The sun crossed the sky and gradually slipped into the sea.

Then they heard heavy footsteps and instantly awoke. A huge shadow fell across the entrance to the cave, blocking out the last of the daylight. It was Polyphemus, the giant. He was known to the Greeks as one of the Cyclops, a race of giants with a single eye in the middle of their foreheads. The men fled terrified into the darkest corner of the cave, where they hid from sight.

At first the Cyclops did not see them. He drove his sheep and goats into the cave and prepared for his night's rest. First he turned to a flat stone that lay at the cave's entrance. It was so large and heavy that twenty-four teams of horses could not have dragged it away. The Cyclops picked it up effortlessly and dropped it across the doorway. The Greeks were trapped. They could not escape.

The Cyclops then milked his goats and sheep, filling the bowls to the brim. He threw wood on the fire. By its light he caught sight of Odysseus and his men.

'You are strangers!' boomed the giant, with a voice like thunder echoing around the mountains. 'Who are you and where do you come from?'

Odysseus spoke up. 'We are Greeks,' he said. 'We are sailing to our homes. In the name of the gods let us go peacefully on our way.'

The Cyclops roared with laughter. 'My people do not care about your gods.'

Suddenly he reached out with his huge hands and grasped two of the Greeks. He tore the men to pieces, toasted them on the fire and ate them. Odysseus and the remaining ten men watched in horror. They could do nothing.

When the giant finished his meal, he drank a bowl of milk and lay down to sleep among his sheep. Odysseus drew his sword from its sheath. Now was the time to kill the Cyclops. But he drew back. How could he and his men move the huge stone that lay across the entrance to the cave? Once all the cheeses had been eaten, they would die of hunger, trapped in the cave. So they hid in a corner and waited for daybreak to come.

Next morning the giant awoke, stretched himself, snatched two more of the Greeks, tore them to pieces and ate them. Again he milked his goats and sheep and collected them together at the mouth of the cave. He lifted the stone clear and drove out the animals to graze on the green hills. Turning, he replaced the stone, laughing as he did so, and blocking off the escape of the Greeks. Odysseus and the remaining eight men could hear Polyphemus whistling merrily as he led the sheep and goats to their pastures.

The Greeks were in despair. 'What can we do?' they asked Odysseus. 'We will all die, two by two.'

Odysseus was famous for his cunning. In the past he had tricked many enemies. He now laid his plans to defeat the Cyclops. In the cave the Greeks found a tree trunk as tall as a ship's mast which the giant carried as a shepherd's staff. Odysseus told his men to draw their knives and to cut off a piece about a man's height. They sharpened one end to a fine point as if making a shaft for a spear. They held this point in the fire to harden it. After it cooled, they hid the sharpened spear under leaves and branches. Then they sat down to await the return of the Cyclops.

As the sun set, Polyphemus came home. He moved the door stone and drove his sheep and goats into the cave. He blocked the entrance and sat down to milk his animals, just as before. Then he reached out and seized two men. He dashed their heads against the rocks and ate them. Now there were only six Greeks and Odysseus left.

The Greeks had brought some of their strong wine with them. Odysseus filled a bowl and offered it to the giant. The Cyclops drank deeply and smacked his lips. He had never tasted wine as sparkling as this.

'More! More!' he demanded. Odysseus filled the bowl for a second time. Polyphemus emptied it. 'Tell me your name, stranger,' he called out, 'for I can offer presents too.'

Odysseus filled the bowl for the third time. Again the giant drained it.

'My name is Nobody,' said Odysseus. 'And what gift will you offer to Nobody?'

10

The Cyclops laughed cruelly. 'Your gift, stranger, is this. I will eat the others first and Nobody last of all.' But the wine had made him drowsy and soon he fell into a deep drunken sleep.

Odysseus and his men lifted the sharp stake and pushed it into the fire. It glowed with heat. The men carried the stake towards the sleeping Cyclops and with a fierce thrust they drove it into the giant's single eye. As the eye hissed like red-hot iron dipped in cold water, Odysseus twisted the spear. The Greeks ran to hide in the furthest corner of the cave as the giant leaped to his feet screaming with the pain. He flung himself from one side of the cave to the other, shouting at the top of his voice.

Other giants, hearing the screams, ran up to the cave's entrance and called out to the Cyclops.

'Why do you shout out?' they asked. 'We cannot sleep. Are robbers attacking you?'

The Cyclops called back to them: 'Nobody is here! Nobody has tricked me! Nobody has blinded me!'

The giants laughed. 'If nobody is there, then you are safe, Polyphemus.' And they returned to their own caves. Now it was the turn of the cunning Odysseus to laugh.

In the morning the blind Cyclops could tell by the bleating of his sheep that they wanted to leave the cave. He moved the door stone but sat in the doorway, groping for the men with his huge hands. They still could not escape, for if they tried to run past him, the giant would seize and eat them.

Odysseus tied the sheep together in threes. Under each of the middle sheep he tied one of his men. He chose the biggest ram for himself and clung beneath it, hanging on tightly to the woolly fleece.

As the sheep passed him, the Cyclops ran his hands over the backs of the animals, feeling for the Greeks. But he did not find the men slung underneath the sheep. The last one to go through the entrance was the biggest ram. The giant stopped it and stroked its back. Odysseus held his breath. Would the giant find him?

Polyphemus let the ram go. Outside the cave Odysseus dropped off and untied his men. They ran to their ship, driving the sheep before them. Hurriedly, they set sail, away from the land of the giants. As they sailed away, Odysseus shouted at the top of his voice at Polyphemus who was still sitting at the mouth of the cave, feeling for the Greeks.

'Cyclops! Do not tell your friends that you were blinded by Nobody. Tell them the truth. You were blinded by Odysseus of Greece!'

In a great rage Polyphemus seized rocks and threw them into the sea, showering the Greeks with the spray. For a time the ships were washed back towards the mainland, and Odysseus had to steer carefully to escape. The Cyclops fell on his knees and prayed to the gods to take revenge on the cunning Odysseus. The gods, feeling sorry for the blind Cyclops, listened to his prayers. And among the gods there were enemies of the crafty Odysseus. So before he reached his homeland, the King had to face many more perils and dangerous adventures.

Robin Hood

At one time thick forests covered a large part of England. In one of them, Sherwood Forest near Nottingham, lived a daring outlaw called Robin Hood. He had quarrelled with the Sheriff of Nottingham and had taken to the woods as an outlaw. He gathered around him a group of men who like himself had fallen out with the law. Together this band of men robbed wealthy travellers who rode through the forest. It is said that they stole from the rich to give to the poor. Nevertheless, these outlaws still managed to keep their own wooden chests full of gold and silver coins. Certainly, Robin did not rob peasants, farmers and ordinary folk but he had no liking for rich churchmen (such as bishops, abbots and the like) who at that time often lived in fine style.

One day Robin was out hunting in the forest with Little John (so called because of his large size) when they saw a knight, with sad face and slow pace, ride along the forest track. They jumped down in front of him.

'Will you dine with us in the forest?' Robin asked.

The knight's face brightened. 'I shall be very glad to sit down and eat with outlaws,' he replied, 'for they are free men. I am at liberty now but in a few days I will be as poor as any man in England. And I am sure that a dungeon awaits me.'

They led him to their forest home and sat down among the trees to eat venison and game poached from the Sheriff's land. The mysterious knight ate and drank heartily, and at the end of the meal Robin suggested that he might now pay something for it.

The knight was embarrassed. 'In my saddle-bag there are ten shillings,' he said, quietly. 'Take it all, for I have no more.'

Little John tipped the coins on to the grass. 'It is true, Robin, the knight is as poor as a mouse.'

'My name is Richard of the Lea,' said the stranger. 'I have a son who in fair battle killed a knight from Lancashire and his squire. They had powerful friends, and my son was seized and cast into prison. To save him from death I gave all my money. I also had to pledge my land to the Abbot of St Mary's Abbey in York. And to-morrow I must repay the money I owe to the Abbot or lose my lands and castle to him.'

'And can you pay him?' asked Robin.

'I have nothing but the ten shillings that you see before you,' said the knight.

'And what do you owe?'

'Four hundred gold pieces.'

'You shall not leave the forest empty-handed,' said Robin.

Little John went away and returned with four hundred gold coins taken from their secret hoard. He placed them in Sir Richard's saddle-bag.

One of Robin's men, Will Scarlet, spoke up. 'The knight's clothes are threadbare. Can we not give him a new surcoat, tunic and boots?'

Bewildered by his good fortune, Sir Richard of the Lea set off in his new clothes. Little John went along with him as his squire, and the knight promised Robin that he would return to the greenwood in twelve months with four hundred gold pounds to pay his debt to the outlaws.

Next day the Abbot of St Mary's Abbey sat with his prior, awaiting the arrival of Sir Richard.

'Unless the debt is repaid by midday, Sir Richard's land will be mine,' the Abbot said with satisfaction. He walked impatiently back and forth across the room, hoping the hours would quickly pass. But a moment or two before midday Sir Richard and Little John rode into the courtyard of the abbey.

The Abbot frowned. 'Where is my money?' he demanded, angrily.

The knight saw the greedy eyes of the prior dart to the heavy bag that Little John flung to the floor.

'You cannot have another day. There must be four hundred pounds in that bag if you are not to lose your lands,' said the Abbot, crossly.

Smiling, Sir Richard opened the bag and poured the shining gold pieces on to a table.

'Take your money, sir abbot,' he chuckled. 'And count it carefully. But the prior and your monks, with my squire here, will be witnesses that the debt is fully paid.'

Followed by Little John, grinning fit to burst, Sir Richard strode from the abbey, bid farewell to his squire and returned to his castle where he told the tale to his happy wife.

Twelve months to the day Robin Hood and his outlaws waited in the same forest dell for Sir Richard. He had promised to return the four hundred pounds by midday, but time passed and there was no sign of the knight.

Robin shrugged. 'Perhaps he will not come. Then we must search for him.'

They made their way to the path that ran through the woods, and in a short time a group of people came in sight. At the head of the column were two monks; behind them came servants leading packhorses weighed down with heavy loads; and in the rear were soldiers armed with swords.

'There are over fifty men there,' whispered Will Scarlet.

'Then the prize must be worthy of such a guard,' said Robin. He stepped out into the path of the cavalcade.

'Wait!' he shouted. 'Did you not know that all who pass along this path must pay a toll. The Master of the Forest demands it.'

'And who is this Master?' one of the monks asked.

'You see him standing before you,' Robin bowed. 'Let me introduce him to you – Robin Hood at your service!'

'A thief and a rogue,' declared the monk. He made a sign to the soldiers, but Robin's men stepped out from their hiding-places in the trees with their bows bent and arrows pointing. The men-at-arms dropped their swords.

'The price of the toll is herewith doubled,' Robin announced, laughing. 'Let us see what treasure they have brought us.'

Little John emptied the saddlebags and counted the treasure.

'Eight hundred gold pieces,' he reported.

'And who pays this rich toll?' asked Robin.

The monk looked glumly at him. 'The Abbot of St Mary's,' he replied.

'Well, now,' Robin declared. 'We await four hundred pounds from Sir Richard. But then we receive a gift of eight hundred pounds from our friend the Abbot, a just reward, perhaps, for our patience. Return to your abbey, master monk, and tell the Abbot that the outlaws of Sherwood Forest thank him for his generosity.'

In a furious rage the two monks and their men-at-arms galloped away, the laughter of Robin Hood ringing in their ears. Shortly afterwards Sir Richard of the Lea rode up to repay his debt.

'Keep your money, Sir Richard,' Robin told him. 'I have been paid twofold by the generous Abbot of St Mary's.'

'Then I thank you,' said Sir Richard. 'But I have one gift that you must accept.' He gave the outlaw chief a hundred fine new bows and a hundred sheaves of peacock-feathered arrows. Robin was very pleased with the present.

'There is an archery contest at Nottingham,'

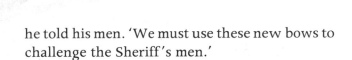

he told his men. 'We must use these new bows to challenge the Sheriff's men.'

Disguised as ordinary yeomen, the outlaws entered the competition, and Robin's skill with the bow won him the main prize, a silver arrow. Pulling his cap down over his eyes, the outlaw mounted the steps of the pavilion to receive his prize. To his dismay the Abbot of St Mary's stood next to the Sheriff.

'By the saints, it is Robin Hood,' he shouted.

Robin did not wait to argue. He ran with his men towards the forest. Pursued by the Sheriff's men-at-arms, a running battle developed, and archers from both sides fell wounded.

As the outlaws reached the safety of the trees, an arrow caught Little John in the knee. Much, the miller's son, picked up Little John and carried him on his shoulder. But he was no lightweight, and Much was soon staggering and stumbling.

'We shall never reach the deepest woods alive,' gasped Will Scarlet.

'It is only half a mile to Sir Richard's castle. He will surely give us shelter,' Robin answered. He did not wish to bring trouble on Sir Richard, but the Sheriff's soldiers were close behind them.

Sir Richard had been watching from the battlements of his castle. As soon as the outlaws were inside the castle gates, he drew up the drawbridge. Baffled and angry, the Sheriff shouted to him to open up, but by this time Robin was dining in the Great Hall of the castle. The outlaws stayed a few days, long enough for Little John's wound to heal, and then they returned to the forest.

The Sheriff and the Abbot, meanwhile, had gone to London. They told the King that something had to be done about the insolent rogues in Sherwood Forest. The King promised to ride north in a few weeks' time, and the two men returned to Nottingham. But the Sheriff could not wait. He planned a trap for the outlaws. While Sir Richard was out hunting, the Sheriff's men surrounded the knight and took him to a dungeon in Nottingham castle. Sir Richard's wife rode into the forest to ask for Robin's help.

'I beg you, do not let them hang my husband from the battlements,' she implored.

Robin collected a hundred men, and in disguise they made their way to Nottingham. The Sheriff and his men were waiting for them in the streets of the town. They fought in the narrow lanes, while the townsfolk trembled behind locked doors. At the end of a long day the Sheriff lay dead and Sir Richard was free. But he did not dare to return to his castle: now he had to roam with the outlaws in the forest.

16

As soon as the King heard the news, he set off with a good force of knights and archers to comb the forest. For two weeks, in a cat-and-mouse game, the outlaws dodged the King's soldiers.

'We shall never catch this villain,' said the King in disgust.

An old forester, standing at the King's side, spoke up: 'I can show you a way to meet Robin Hood.'

'Tell me, quickly,' said the King.

'Take only five knights, all in disguise as monks, and go into the very deepest part of the forest. The outlaws cannot resist an abbot or a monk.'

The King laughed, donned an abbot's habit and set off. Sure enough, as the little group of 'monks' made their way through the woods, men dressed in Lincoln green tunics dropped down from the trees. Their leader put his hand on the bridle of the King's horse.

'You are a brave man,' said Robin. 'Perhaps, sir abbot, you bring us more gold from your hoard.'

'I have only forty pieces,' said the King.

'I shall have twenty to give to the poor,' answered Robin. 'You may keep twenty for your expenses but you must take your dinner with us. The King will provide the venison from his land, though he does not know it.'

After they had eaten, Robin Hood arranged an archery contest. The King marvelled at their skill.

'Your archers are far better than the King's men,' he said.

'Will you try your skill?' Robin asked the abbot.

The King was one of the best soldiers in England. He shot six arrows at the target but could not match Robin's hits. As he fired his last arrow, the King's cowl fell back to show his long brown hair.

Sir Richard gasped. 'It is our lord, the King of England.' He fell on his knees. All of Robin's men knelt down.

'Will you have mercy on us, sire?' Robin asked.

The King looked down at them. 'You should all hang from the battlements,' he told them. 'But England needs soldiers such as you. I invite you to join the King's service. If you will return the gold and silver in your coffers to the owners, I shall grant you a pardon so that you may return to your homes. And, for those who wish it, I offer service in the King's army.'

Robin Hood and his outlaws thus left the forest, swore loyalty to the King and for some years lived at peace. But the King died, and a tyrant took his place. Before long Robin and his comrades were back in the forest, enjoying the old free life, poaching the King's deer, stealing from abbots and other rich churchmen, helping the poor and in other ways making a nuisance of themselves. This went on for some years until Robin was finally betrayed.

In one of his many fights Robin was wounded. With Little John he visited Ursula, the abbess of a convent in Yorkshire. Robin did not know that she had promised to kill him if the outlaw ever came into her power. She told Robin to lie down on a bed and gave him a drink to soothe the pain. He drank deeply and slept. While he did so she cut a vein in his wrist. When he awoke he found his life-blood dripping away in a bowl beside the bed. With the last of his strength he dragged himself to the window and blew on his horn. Little John, who had been keeping guard beyond the wall of the convent, ran to his leader.

When Little John saw Robin near to death, he vowed to burn down the convent.

'We have never harmed a woman,' Robin whispered. 'Do not do so now.' He pointed to his bow. 'I shall fire my last arrow. Wherever it rests, bury me in that spot.'

He had little strength left—just enough to bend the bow and send an arrow out of the window, across the wall and into the long grass of the woods.

'Bury me there,' he muttered with his last breath. And so, at the end, Robin Hood came to rest among the trees that had given him shelter for many years when he was both the King's enemy and his friend.

18

Cuchulain, the Hound of Ulster

Maeve was the Queen of Connacht in Ireland. She boasted to her husband that her treasure was far greater than his. She had flocks of sheep, beautiful golden drinking mugs and clothes covered in jewels. But Ailell, her husband, possessed a great bull with white horns that shone in the moonlight. The bull had the strength of fifty ordinary bulls, and all men and animals feared it.

Queen Maeve called to her messengers. 'Search every field in Ireland,' she told them, 'until you find such a bull. Then it will be made to fight the White-Horned Bull to see who is the master.'

In the north of the country, in Ulster, the messengers found a champion. It was the Brown Bull of the village of Cooley. The Queen's messenger offered fifty cows and a chariot to the farmer for the bull, but the farmer refused.

When the news was brought to Maeve, she cried out in anger, 'I will send my army to Ulster to take this Brown Bull of Cooley by force!'

Her greatest soldier, Fergus, replied in a low voice, 'Beware, Queen, for these bulls are gods and they will stir up a mighty war with killing and burning.'

But the Queen took no notice and led her army out on the road to Cooley. Fierce men in long kilts, their spears held ready, followed their Queen. She rode in her chariot, her long yellow hair hanging to her shoulders, a sword at her side.

At that time Ulster was ruled by King Conor, the leader of a band of warriors called the Red Branch Knights. But mysteriously all of the Knights fell sick and could not stop Queen Maeve's army. Only one warrior, young Cuchulain, who was at home with his father, escaped the sickness.

'I will stand alone before the men of Connacht,' Cuchulain said. He went into a wood and pulled down a young oak tree. He stripped it of its branches and carried it to the river where Queen Maeve's army would cross. He rammed the tree into the mud of the river. Then he hid from sight.

Four men from the Queen's army rode up. Cuchulain leaped from his hiding place and struck off their heads. He placed their heads on the pole in the river and again hid from sight.

When Queen Maeve came to the river, she saw the heads. 'Who would do such a thing?' she asked in horror.

'A great warrior or a giant,' said Fergus. 'For who else would have the strength?'

'We will trick the giant,' said the Queen. 'Do not cross yet. We will keep to the Connacht bank. The giant will go away, thinking we are afraid to cross.'

So on they went through marshes and snow. No one caught sight of Cuchulain, but soldiers disappeared in ones and twos, never to be seen again.

The Queen grew nervous. 'We hear strange tales of a youth by the name of Cuchulain,' she said, 'who is famous for his warlike powers. Could he be leading a band against us?'

'Cuchulain is but seventeen years of age,' Fergus replied. 'I knew him as a very young boy when he had the strength equal to ten men.'

'I have heard of this boy,' Maeve said. 'He is called the Hound of Ulster. How did he come to have that name?'

'Years ago,' Fergus began, 'King Conor and his Knights stopped by a village to watch boys at a game. One little boy sent a dozen balls flying between the goal-posts. The King was so pleased that he told the small boy to come to his great feast that evening. But as the boy made his way across the fields, he was stopped by a huge watch-dog with the strength and fury of a hundred ordinary dogs.'

Fergus stopped for a moment as he remembered the fearsome beast. 'With jaws as wide as a gate, the dog rushed to tear the boy to pieces. But as the dog sprang at him, the boy caught the great hound by the throat and dashed its brains against the gatepost. King Conor was amazed, and from that moment named the boy Cuchulain, the Hound of Ulster. By that name he has been known ever since.'

'I must see this young man,' declared the Queen. 'Send my messengers out to meet him.'

Maeve offered Cuchulain great areas of land in Connacht if he would join her army and fight King Conor. But Cuchulain, who came out into the open, refused all offers.

When the Queen saw him, she was amazed. 'He is young, as you say, scarcely seventeen summers, and has one weapon, a sling. What can a few stones do against my army?'

The fighting began again, and one evening as the Queen sat outside her tent a stone flew through the air and knocked her pet bird from her shoulder. A second stone hit the squirrel that sat on her other shoulder. She ran to her tent and took shelter.

'Go to Cuchulain,' said the Queen, 'and find out what he will accept from us.'

'I will fight your champions,' said the Hound of Ulster, 'one at a time.'

At first Maeve kept to the agreement and sent her warriors out one by one. Cuchulain stood on the bank of the river and whirled his sling. Before the warriors could reach him, they fell dead from a sling stone.

'Send a hundred warriors,' said the Queen.

Now Cuchulain fought his hardest battle. A hundred men stormed across the river. The sling circled above Cuchulain's head again and again. In twos and threes he slew men, leaving their bodies in heaps around the river. But the Hound of Ulster was himself wounded by the swords of his enemies. When night came, the fighting ended. Weary and wounded, Cuchulain lay on a hillside and looked down into the enemy camp. A thousand men were polishing their spears and swords. In despair he stood on the hill and let out a blood-curdling call. So loud was the cry that all the demons, goblins, elves and other spirits of the hills answered him with their yells. Maddened by fear, the Connacht soldiers rose to their feet and ran here and there, stabbing at shadows. Many men died in the confusion from wounds given by their own troops.

'I will trick this warrior,' Queen Maeve cried in a great rage. She left the fires of the camp burning, and most of her army stayed by the river bank. She led a group of her best warriors to the village of Cooley and captured the Brown Bull. Cuchulain, weary and wounded, could do nothing. He could not be in two places at once. He did not have those magic powers. As he lay injured on the hillside, a man dressed in a green cloak fastened with a silver brooch came towards him out of the mist.

'Who are you?' asked Cuchulain. 'Another enemy?'

'I have a magic ointment,' said the stranger, 'to spread on your wounds.'

It was the sun god. He sang a tune that put Cuchulain to sleep for three days. The stranger laid herbs that healed and oils that caused the cuts to disappear on Cuchulain's wounds. When Cuchulain awoke, the sun god had disappeared, but he was refreshed, ready for the fight again. When the battle started, Cuchulain found that he had a new power. He could turn in his own skin, so that his feet and hands faced one way, with his head and chest facing another.

When Maeve returned and started the battle again, she despaired of ever defeating Cuchulain. Her wise men and captains of war called with one voice: 'Send Ferdia against the Hound! It is your last chance of victory.'

Ferdia had taken no part in the fighting. He, the greatest soldier in Maeve's army, secretly admired Cuchulain and hoped he would not fall in battle.

Queen Maeve called Ferdia to her tent. 'I can offer you lands and treasure to fight Cuchulain,' she said, 'but you would refuse all of these offers. But there is one reward that you will not refuse. I give you my beautiful daughter in marriage if you will fight Cuchulain.'

Ferdia hesitated, because he loved her daughter. 'I was a friend of Cuchulain's in his boyhood,' he told her, 'and now I cannot break that bond.'

Queen Maeve called the whole army together. 'Hear this!' she shouted to them. 'I tell you that your champion Ferdia is a coward.'

Ferdia returned to his tent. Next morning he rose early and prepared his chariot and his weapons. When he reached the river, he called out to Cuchulain on the opposite bank.

'It is said that I am a coward. Do not let us exchange words, only weapons.'

They began with small spears. They flung them back and forth, until they buzzed like bees in the sun. When night came they rested and dressed each other's wounds. Cuchulain gave Ferdia some of the magic herbs to heal his cuts.

Next day they fought from their chariots with broad spears. And again at night they stopped, rested and tended each other's wounds. On the third morning Cuchulain saw that Ferdia could scarcely lift his sword. He called out that they would end the fighting. But Ferdia declared that he would not be called a coward. So they fought again. Towards the end of the day Cuchulain sent a spear that pierced Ferdia's armour and dug deep into his flesh.

'The end is come,' whispered Ferdia, and died.

Cuchulain could fight no longer. Queen Maeve prepared to ride across Ulster which she promised to destroy with fire and sword. But the long sleep and the sickness was lifted by the gods from the Red Branch Knights. King Conor gathered his warriors around him and marched south to meet the Queen. When they reached the river where Cuchulain lay and saw his wounds, the Knights bound him to his bed with ropes.

'We shall take over the fighting from you, Cuchulain,' said Conor, 'for you have done enough for Ulster.'

The men of Connacht were now very tired and, since they had the Brown Bull of Cooley, they wished to be home. So they left the battlefield and travelled back to Connacht. When the Brown Bull saw the wild country of his enemies, he let out a bellow that rolled like thunder round the hills. The White-Horned Bull heard it and lifted up his great head to listen. No other bull had ever dared to say more than a quiet 'moo'. He tore the ground with his hoof and tossed his head angrily. What cow or bull dared to raise its voice so loud?

The men of Connacht put the two bulls in the same field. The eyes of the bulls blazed like fire as they looked at each other. Their cheeks and nostrils swelled. They ran at each other and crashed with a noise that shook the hills where Maeve and her husband stood to watch the struggle. All day the two bulls chased, butted and gored at each other. They fought through the night, and no one could sleep through it. As daylight came, Maeve saw one of the bulls climb a hill, the other bull impaled on its horns. Which of the bulls had won the victory? A great roar came from the bull. They knew then that it was the Brown Bull of Cooley that had won. The bull tossed his horns and flung the flesh of the White-Horned Bull over all Ireland.

Breaking free of the field, the Brown Bull set off for home. When he saw the hills of Cooley, such joy rose in him that he charged at them. He drove his forehead at a mountain and a stream of blood rushed from his mouth. His heart burst within him, and he died.

And so the story of the Brown Bull of Cooley ended. As for Cuchulain, he returned to his farm. Seven years later he took to the battlefield again to fight the army of Queen Maeve, but that is another story.

Rama and the King of the Demons

In India long ago there were many kings. Each kingdom had fine cities with high walls and strong gates, guarded by soldiers of the king. One of these cities was ruled by a king called Dasa Ratha. He lived in a great palace, dressed in silks and jewels and was greatly loved by his people.

Dasa Ratha had four sons, strong and handsome boys who rode out hunting with him. Rama, the eldest, was the best shot with his bow and arrow, the best rider on horseback and the strongest of the princes in battle.

But the king also had three wives, as was the custom in India in those days. The youngest

queen, Kaikeyi, was jealous of Rama. She twisted and turned the old king's mind and reminded him that when he had been ill she had nursed him and saved his life. For her reward she demanded that Rama should be banished from the kingdom for fourteen years and that her son should take his place.

Dasa Ratha pleaded and argued. But Kaikeyi would not give in.

'Do you remember, O Great King,' she said, 'that long ago when I saved your life you promised me any wish?'

'I remember,' replied Dasa Ratha, sadly.

'I claim your promise now,' she went on. 'Send Rama away from this palace.'

Rama put aside his silk clothes, his jewelled sword. He dressed as a poor man. Sita, his beautiful young wife, said that she would go with him.

His young brother Lakshman could not bear to be parted. So all three went into the dark forest. And Dasa Ratha, heart-broken, died within a year, leaving Kaikeyi's son as ruler.

In the forest they dressed in clothes made from skins and from tree bark. They lived in bamboo huts and ate berries and wild fruit. Holy men visited them. One of the holy men gave Rama a bow with a quiver of magic arrows. The animals of the jungle became their friends. They were very poor but happy. Then danger suddenly came upon them.

One day, while hunting in the forest, King Ravana of Lanka saw Sita gathering berries. He fell in love with her, and since he was king of the demons, he sent evil spirits to capture her. Rama fought them off with his magic arrows until the forest ran red with their blood.

Ravana could take the shape of an animal or a human, so he decided to trap Sita by trickery. A few days later Sita sat outside the hut, working flowers into her hair. Suddenly, a golden deer appeared at the edge of the forest. The beautiful and strange animal shone in the sunlight. Its wistful eyes stared directly into hers, imprisoning her eyes and her mind. She felt a great longing to stroke the deer. She ran after it, but the animal danced away from her.

'Rama!' she called. 'Come here, quickly!'

Rama ran from the hut, smiling at her.

'I want it!' Sita gasped, entranced. 'I must have the deer.'

Rama moved after the animal which skipped away on its golden feet.

Calling on Lakshman to stay behind to guard Sita, Rama gathered his bow and ran after the deer. The forest was still, silent. Not a leaf moved. Suddenly, away in the forest, Sita and Lakshman heard a cry of pain. Rama's voice came to them out of the trees.

'Lakshman! Help me!' cried the voice. 'I am attacked by a demon.'

'It is a trick,' said Lakshman. 'Take no notice. Rama has killed a thousand demons.'

But Sita was afraid. 'You are a coward,' she accused Lakshman, unfairly.

Lakshman was horrified. He did not know that Sita's mind had been twisted by the deer's powerful eyes. He picked up his bow and arrows. But before he left he drew a line of protection around the hut.

'Do not cross it,' he told her, 'for anyone or anything that might happen.'

Lakshman had been right. The deer was one of Ravana's demons in disguise. Rama chased it for miles. Tiring, he shot an arrow to wound and slow the animal. But as the blood spurted from its leg, the deer turned into a demon and imitated his voice perfectly. Rama turned and raced back through the jungle towards the hut. But he was too late to save Sita.

Only a moment after Lakshman had left her, an old man stepped out of the trees. Gentle, holy and frail, he held out a begging bowl towards Sita. She crossed the line to place some food in the old man's bowl.

The kind face changed, becoming crafty and evil. The bent body straightened, and the arms of the old man turned to steel as they gripped Sita.

'I am Ravana, King of Lanka, Lord of the Demon World,' he said. 'You will be my wife. I shall carry you to my palace beyond the sea.'

To Sita's horror ten heads grew out of Ravana's body. A chariot appeared. She was pushed into it, and they flew up into the sky. An eagle, friendly to Rama, tried to stop them. Ravana stabbed the eagle which fell to earth.

Rama and Lakshman returned together. Sita had gone. They searched through the forest and found a dying eagle. The bird whispered one word before it died – 'Ravana'. The brothers set out again on a longer search. They wandered over hills and mountains, along the streams and rivers and through the jungle. Eventually they climbed the highest mountain and met Hanuman, the king of the monkey people.

'We will help you to search for Sita,' Hanuman promised.

The monkeys were divided into bands and sent out into the forest. Months passed, and all the monkeys returned, shaking their heads when Rama asked them if they had found Sita. Only Hanuman had not returned. He went south to the very edge of India. Beyond lay the sparkling sea with an island in the distance. He did not know, but the island was Lanka, the kingdom of Ravana. As he was about to return, a bird swooped down and told Hanuman that a chariot with a beautiful, weeping woman had flown overhead some weeks before.

Hamuman raced to tell Rama the news. An army gathered together, an army of monkeys, bears, squirrels and other animals. They marched through the forest to the southern shore. But how could they cross to Lanka? The squirrels set to work, cutting down trees. The bears laid rocks in the sea and covered them with the trees. Soon a bridge began to stretch towards the island.

'I will go ahead,' said Hanuman, 'and look for Sita. I shall raise her spirits by telling her that you are nearby.'

As king of the monkeys Hanuman possessed magic powers. In one jump he cleared the sea to land on the island. He found Sita closely guarded. By climbing and hiding in a tree he could speak to her. She gave him a pin from her hair to carry to Rama. But as he was making his way to the coast, he was captured and taken to Ravana.

Bound with rope, Hanuman was carried to the palace. As a cruel punishment to amuse the people, an oil-soaked rag was tied to his tail and set alight. To be able to watch him dance in pain Ravana ordered the monkey's release from the ropes. Hanuman leaped to the rooftops, dragging the length of burning cloth behind him. He went from one rooftop to another, setting fire to the houses. Soon, flames and smoke rose from

28

the burning city. But his tail hurt, and to ease the pain he put the end of his tail in his mouth. The fire went out, but the inside of his mouth turned black. This is why monkeys have black roofs to their mouths to this day.

Hanuman escaped from the city and returned to Rama to tell him that he must hurry. Rama led his army towards the great gateway. He took the precaution of fixing a mirror to the front of his shield. One of Ravana's generals had only one eye. The eye normally remained tightly closed, for when it opened and looked the object it rested on was burnt to ashes. Ravana told the general to stare at Rama. The general opened his eye, the mirror caught and returned the look, and the general fell to the ground, burnt to a cinder.

The army of the demon king and the army of the animals fought a long and bitter battle. Many were killed on both sides. Ravana, with his ten heads and his magic powers, thought he would win. The mountains echoed with the clang of weapons, and the ground trembled beneath their feet. Rama's magic bow and arrows killed many of the demon king's champions, and an arrow pierced Ravana's chest, forcing him to leave the battle.

Ravana now called for the help of his son. He was a giant who slept for six months and awoke for a day. It was difficult to rouse him, but when the giant stumbled into battle, he trampled fifty monkeys under each of his huge feet. He snatched up Hanuman to eat him, but the monkey tore off one of the giant's ears and ran off with it. The bleeding and angry giant charged the monkey army, and it needed all of Rama's magic to stop him. Twenty arrows thudded into the giant's flesh before he fell to the ground with a crash that rocked the city.

With his wounds mended, Ravana returned. But he had no more sons, no more generals, no more magic powers. He emerged from the city and challenged Rama to a duel. He flung javelins, fired magic arrows and sent a black cloud to hide a shower of poison darts. Each of the weapons was turned aside by Rama's shield or sword.

Finally, Rama picked up one of Ravana's death darts and fired it from his bow. It struck the demon king. As he fell dead, evil spirits all over the world shrieked and died with him.

'Bring Sita to me,' commanded Rama.

Joyfully, Sita left her prison and ran to meet Rama.

'Have you been faithful to me?' Rama asked.

'Yes, and I will prove it,' Sita answered.

The city was on fire. A huge fire burned before them. Sita walked up to the flames and stood at the edge of the fire.

'To prove my faithfulness I shall walk through the fire,' she said.

While the whole army watched in silence, Sita stepped into the flames and disappeared. Then, without a burn on her clothing or her body, she emerged from the terrible fire.

'Let us return to the city of my father,' Rama announced, 'for the fourteen years have passed. And you, Sita, are truly a queen.'

And so Rama, Sita and Lakshman returned to their own city where everyone turned out to welcome them, bearing Rama's sandals on a royal elephant and carrying bowls of flowers for Sita.

Siegfried and the Ice Queen

Sitting high up on a castle wall, a young man dreamed of adventure. The youth's name was Siegfried, and he was the son of the king of a peaceful country where people were good and there were no princesses to be saved or dragons to be fought. Siegfried was restless and he made his father very sad by leaving his country to search for adventure, fame and treasure. Travelling by horse and by ship, he visited many lands. He fought giants and dwarfs with magic powers. He found caves full of gold. He slew the terrible Dragon of the Night. Shortly after his return home from one voyage, he heard stories about the land of Burgundy ruled over by King Gunther. In this fair kingdom lived the King's sister, Kriemhild, a lovely princess. Minstrels travelled to many lands to sing of her great beauty, and Siegfried, with many other young men, set off for Burgundy to see her.

Siegfried, being a prince, was taken to the court. He immediately fell in love with the beautiful Kriemhild and wanted to marry her.

'No! I cannot think of weddings!' King Gunther cried. 'We are attacked by barbarians on all sides of Burgundy. You must first prove yourself in battle by my side.'

So Siegfried and his companions went off to war. Armed with his great sword Balmunga, the young prince showed himself to be the greatest warrior on the battlefield, and the Saxons were defeated.

'May I marry your sister?' Siegfried asked, when they had returned to court.

'There is a minstrel come to my court with a tale about a far-off land,' Gunther replied. 'I must hear it.'

The minstrel sang about the Last Land, called Iceland, far away across the dark ocean. Here Queen Brunhilde ruled in a castle surrounded by burning fire. She was waiting for a prince who was as strong as she to come and claim her. The halls of her castle were covered with the shields of kings who had sailed to Iceland and who had been overcome by Queen Brunhilde in battle.

'Is there really such a warlike queen?' asked Gunther in amazement.

'Yes. I have heard the story from the minstrels,' Siegfried agreed.

'And is she, as the song tells it, stronger than any man?'

Again Siegfried nodded. 'The story is true,' he said.

'My strength is not great enough to win her,' Gunther went on, sadly, 'but I wish to marry her. Siegfried, will you fight for me and win this northern Ice Queen?'

'I will,' replied Siegfried, 'but on one condition. A wife for a wife. I will conquer Brunhilde for you if you will let me marry Kriemhild.'

'Agreed!' laughed Gunther. 'Prepare for a voyage and for two weddings.'

Loaded with supplies, the ships sailed down the river Rhine and into the open seas. For twelve days the sailors saw nothing but the grey sea and sky until Volker, the minstrel, shouted: 'Land! Land! Soon they saw the walls of the castle in the land of ice and snow.

King Gunther dressed himself in his finest

clothes. He wore shining armour, carried a golden shield, and over his shoulders he hung a coat studded with pearls and jewels.

As the ships neared the shore, a group of armed women came to the water's edge, watching and waiting.

'The lady in white is the Queen,' Siegfried said. 'She is the tallest, the most powerful, and she has killed twenty kings.'

As the Burgundians landed, the warriors of the Ice Queen surrounded them. Brunhilde stepped forward. Her helmet glinted like ice under the pale sun. She looked directly at Siegfried.

'I have seen you in a dream,' she said. 'You are King Siegfried. At last you have come.'

'No!' replied Siegfried. 'I am only the humble servant of King Gunther of Burgundy who has come to fight and claim you as his wife.'

Brunhilde turned to Gunther. 'Do you know the law? If you wish to claim me, you must fight me in open battle. First, the trial of the sword. If you are still alive, you will have the trial of the stone.'

As they prepared for battle, Siegfried slipped away to his ship. He put on Tarnkappe, his magic cape. Wearing it, he was invisible. He stood behind Gunther and touched his hand.

'It is I, Siegfried,' he whispered. 'No one can see me. I will stand behind you. Do everything that the Queen asks.'

Gunther and Brunhilde took up their positions a great distance apart. Each held a shield. Brunhilde carried a huge, heavy sword. Slowly, carefully, she raised it above her head and with a mighty heave she flung it at Gunther. Siegfried, hidden by his magic cloak, slipped behind Gunther as the King raised his shield. But not even Siegfried's great strength could halt the hurtling sword. It crashed into the shield and flung both men to the ground.

'Now it is your turn,' whispered Siegfried as they got to their feet. 'But we must not kill her. I wish to go to two weddings. Pick up your sword.'

Gunther held the heavy sword in his hand. Siegfried placed his invisible hands over Gunther's, and the two men whirled the sword above their heads.

The sword flew through the air and slammed into Brunhilde's shield, tearing it in half and knocking her to the ground. Brunhilde's face darkened in anger.

'Now for the stone!' she called out.

She ran to a huge stone that would have needed twelve men to move. She raised it above her head and flung it a great distance. Then she took a leap, landing in the sand of the beach. She marked the place where she landed and stared at Gunther.

Gunther was dismayed. 'I shall never lift the stone,' he said, 'nor be able to make such a leap.'

Siegfried laughed. 'Stand side by side,' he instructed the King. 'Now – lift!'

It took all of Siegfried's great strength to thrust the stone into the air, but it crashed to the ground at a greater distance than the Queen's throw.

'Now,' Siegfried whispered, 'for the jump.' He lifted Gunther in his invisible arms and leaped further than Brunhilde's mark.

The Ice Queen fell to her knees. 'I am beaten!' she cried. 'I have lost! My strength is gone, and I am the servant of the King of Burgundy.'

Siegfried returned to his ship and hid his magic cloak.

'What has happened?' he asked, innocently, on his return to the shore. Brunhilde was weeping bitter tears.

Gunther shouted, his voice echoing around the icy wastes: 'Prepare the ships. We shall return to Burgundy where there will be rejoicing and two weddings.'

As the Burgundians prepared for their departure, Siegfried called for all his friends from the underworld to come forward. He did not trust Brunhilde. He believed that she was plotting against the King. Suddenly, from nowhere, an army of a thousand giants and dwarfs appeared at Siegfried's side. Brunhilde was amazed and

thought that Gunther had magic powers. She realized that she had lost her great battle. The warriors of the Ice Queen wept as she boarded the King's ship and sailed away.

As they sailed up the river Rhine, Gunther showed her the fields, the gardens and orchards of his fair land. His subjects waved and smiled as the ships passed by. But Brunhilde neither laughed nor smiled.

'This will never be my home,' she wept.

Gunther's mother and Kriemhild welcomed the new Queen.

'We will be married in three days,' the King announced.

Throughout the two weddings Brunhilde continued to weep. She watched the games and the sports held in her honour, the dancing and the singing, but always with a sad and gloomy face.

'I hate this place,' she told Gunther. 'And why do you allow that servant to sit at your table and to marry your sister?'

'That is Siegfried,' laughed the King. 'Some day I will tell you about him.'

That evening in their room Gunther spoke angrily to Brunhilde. 'When will the weeping stop?' he demanded.

'Not until I return to my own people!' she replied.

In his rage Gunther struck her. Brunhilde turned on him like a tigress. She flung the King to the floor, tied him up in his belt and hung him from a nail in the wall.

'Put me down! You cannot do this to a king,' Gunther pleaded.

Next morning Brunhilde lifted him down from the nail. Gunther ran to find Siegfried.

'She is a witch!' he cried.

'Nonsense!' said Siegfried. 'You must beat her again, but this time I will help you.'

That night Gunther blew out all the candles in their room. He opened the door, and Siegfried slipped silently into the room. As Gunther crouched in a corner, Siegfried and Brunhilde fought in the darkness until the Queen gave in.

'Do not kill me, Gunther,' she begged, 'for I surrender.'

Bruised and battered, Siegfried crept away, carrying in his hand Brunhilde's jewelled belt which he had torn from her in the struggle.

'Where did you get that belt?' asked Kriemhild when he returned to their room. Siegfried told her the whole story of how he had fought Brunhilde twice, and Kriemhild promised never to tell anyone the secret. But later, at the games, Brunhilde mocked Kriemhild about marrying a servant.

'He is no servant,' Kriemhild replied, proudly. 'He is King Siegfried, who beats barbarian women from across the seas.'

Brunhilde saw the belt at Kriemhild's waist. 'That is my belt!' Suddenly, she understood how she had been tricked. She went to her room and locked the door.

Servants ran to Gunther to tell him what had happened.

'Siegfried is loved by the two women who are dearest to me,' he said, sadly. 'I wish he was dead, but he is stronger than all of us, and the people of my country love him.'

One of Gunther's warriors heard the King. He made a vow to kill Siegfried.

A few days later the men went hunting. Siegfried had skin as hard as armour except for one place on his back. Kriemhild had sewn a patch over this spot. As Siegfried knelt down by a stream to drink from it, the Burgundian warrior plunged his spear through the very centre of the patch. Siegfried fell into the stream and died. The huntsmen returned to Gunther's castle carrying the blood-stained body of the great hero. Kriemhild, weeping, vowed that one day she would be revenged upon the traitor and on her own brother, King Gunther.

Brunhilde waited until darkness fell. Then she secretly placed Siegfried's body on a ship. Alone, she set sail for the Last Land, the country of ice and snow where Siegfried was given a funeral fit for a hero.

King Arthur: the Sword from the Stone

Hundreds of years ago there was a king in Britain called Uther Pendragon. He was a good king, a fierce warrior in battle and a clever and kind man to his people. Much of his power came from one of his wise men, Merlin. For Merlin was a wizard with magic powers. He could read the secrets of men's lives in the stars and he could talk to the creatures of the night and the underworld. He could tell people what would happen in the future, and it was said that he even knew the secrets of Nature.

One day a fierce knight came with his army to attack Uther's castle. In the battle the knight was killed, and Uther pursued the fleeing soldiers to their castle of Tintagel in Cornwall. The moment that Uther saw the dead knight's wife, Igraine, he fell in love with her.

'I must marry her,' he told his men.

But Merlin's face grew anxious. 'No good can ever come of such a marriage,' he said to the King. 'For you have committed a terrible deed in killing Igraine's husband.'

'I care nothing for old men's tales,' Uther said carelessly. 'Prepare, for we are to be married in six weeks.'

Igraine had a daughter, Morgan le Fay. She, like Merlin, was skilled in magic and could work strange spells like a witch. Morgan swore to have her revenge on Uther and his family for she had dearly loved her father who was now dead. She nursed her hatred secretly in her heart and came with her mother, Igraine, to live in Uther's castle.

Months passed, and Igraine had a son. He was named Arthur. As he lay in his cot, Morgan came to visit the baby boy.

'Is he not beautiful?' Queen Igraine asked her daughter. 'And one day he will be King of all Britain.'

Morgan said nothing. She waited until she was alone with the child, until the shadows of the setting sun crept across the room. Arthur lay in his cot at her mercy.

Morgan ran her fingers over a piece of yellow stone with deep rings of brown – her 'tiger's eye' she called it. The stone glittered as if it had an inner fire. She seemed to be surrounded by a cage of light. She saw a vision of Arthur with a crown on his head. In his hand was a sword. Beside him was gathered a group of knights, seated at a round table. Then the picture faded and reformed. The knights turned into corpses, lying on a battlefield. Arthur, with blood streaming from the jewels in his crown, leaned on his sword.

'Arthur!' said Morgan le Fay softly. 'You will inherit the Kingdom of Death.'

She uttered a curse over the baby as it lay helpless in its cot. Then she slipped away, unseen.

The years passed. Two years after Arthur's birth King Uther died, and Queen Igraine died shortly afterwards. Morgan le Fay married a king in a far-off land. Merlin hoped that she would never return. But with no one to rule Britain the country passed into a state of war. Kings and knights fought among themselves for a piece of land, a castle, a crown. Merlin feared that the baby Arthur would come to harm and

so, wrapping the child in a cloth of gold, he carried him secretly to the castle of a friendly knight.

'Raise him as if he were your own son,' Merlin warned the knight. 'And you will one day be richly rewarded. But tell no one, not even Arthur, that you give shelter to the son of King Uther.'

Arthur grew up to become a powerful young man, a fine horseman who led hunting parties through the forests. From time to time Merlin visited the castle to teach him the duties of a king.

Arthur was puzzled; why should the old wizard take such an interest in him, an ordinary knight's son? He shrugged his shoulders, listened to what Merlin had to say, and then ran off into the forest in pursuit of deer or a wild boar.

One day, when Arthur was fourteen years old, a stone suddenly appeared before a church in London. Merlin's magic had placed it there. On the stone stood an anvil, and thrust deep into the anvil was a sword. In gold letters a message was written: 'He who draws this sword from the stone is the rightful King of Britain.'

Thousands of knights came to London to try to pull the sword from the stone. They all failed.

Soon afterwards a tournament was held in the city. Arthur travelled there with Sir Kay, his best friend. Sir Kay was to take part in the jousts, and Arthur would hold his lance, polish his shield and sword and lead his horse. On the morning of the tournament they hurried to the big field where it was to be held. To his dismay Sir Kay found that he had left his sword at the inn.

'Ride back to the inn and fetch it,' Sir Kay told Arthur.

But the inn was closed: everyone had gone to the tournament. Arthur rode through the streets of London, trying to borrow a sword. But the streets were also deserted. He came to a church, and there, stuck through a stone and an anvil, was a gleaming sword. Arthur did not have time to read the message. He pulled, and the sword came out of the stone like a knife out of butter. He hurried to the tournament field with the sword.

Sir Kay and the knights all gathered around him.

'Show us,' they asked, 'the secret. How did you pull the sword from the stone?'

Everyone returned to the church. Hundreds of people gathered to watch. Arthur pushed the sword into the stone and drew it free again. He replaced it, so that all the knights and kings could try, but only Arthur could draw it from the stone.

'You will be King of Britain,' said Sir Kay.

And all the knights knelt down before Arthur.

'Do not kneel,' he cried out, 'for who am I but an ordinary knight, the brother of Sir Kay.'

Then Sir Kay came forward and told him how he was really King Uther's son. And so, with thousands cheering, Arthur became the King of Britain.

Arthur left the city and took up his place as King. For the next few years Merlin looked after

The King laughed. 'If I had not come when I did, you would be dead, Merlin.'

'Not I, my lord King. I have ways of avoiding death, ways not known to ordinary men.'

'That is a puzzle,' said Arthur, 'for you were near death then.'

'Not as near as you will be before long,' Merlin replied. 'Beware, for there is danger, and also a reward!' And with that strange warning Merlin disappeared.

Arthur rode on but found a knight barring his path.

'All who come this way must fight to pass,' said the knight.

So they fought, charging at each other across the forest clearing. They shattered their lances on each other's shields. Three times they charged, and three times they broke their lances.

him, protecting Arthur from all enemies. Then one day, as the King was riding in the forest, he saw an old man being attacked by three robbers. Arthur charged, and the robbers fled. The King turned to the old man and saw that it was Merlin.

Then they fought on foot, and by misfortune Arthur's sword shattered in his hand.

'The victory is mine,' said the knight. 'Yield or make ready to die.'

'Never!' Arthur replied, and leaped at the knight with his fists. But the knight still had his sword and, knocking off Arthur's helmet, he raised his arm to strike off the King's head.

At that moment Merlin appeared and touched the knight who rolled over in a deep sleep.

'Do not kill him,' cried Arthur, 'for such a warrior should be in my band of knights.'

'He is sleeping,' Merlin replied. 'Did I not tell you to beware of danger?'

'My sword is broken,' said Arthur sadly.

'Come! Follow me,' said Merlin, 'and I will show you a sword greater than any in the kingdom.'

Merlin led the King to the shore of a lake. He raised his arm and pointed. 'See, there is your sword.'

A mist seemed to gather over the surface of the lake. The mist formed into the shape of an arm clothed in white silk. The hand held a sword – and such a sword! The hilt was richly decorated with gold and precious jewels, and the blade flashed as if with an inner flame. Out of the lake rose a young woman in white.

'It is the Lady of the Lake,' said Merlin. 'Speak to her, and she will give you the sword.'

'Lady of the Lake,' said Arthur, 'who owns that sword?'

'The sword is mine, and its name is Excalibur. I will give it to you as a gift. Take it and the scabbard that holds it.'

With these words the Lady of the Lake stepped back into the green waters, and disappeared from view.

'There is a boat,' Merlin said, 'in the willows by the bank. Take it and row out into the lake.'

So Arthur rowed out into the middle of the waters to where the hand still held the sword, sparkling in the sunshine. He took it and the scabbard in his hand, and instantly the arm vanished below the water.

On the shore of the lake Arthur waved Excalibur above his head.

'The sword is a marvel,' said the King, 'for it will kill many enemies.'

'What is the greater gift,' asked Merlin, 'the sword or the scabbard?'

'Why, of course, the sword! Look at its steel, its jewelled hilt.'

Merlin laughed. 'The scabbard is worth ten swords,' he said.

'How can that be?' asked Arthur, puzzled by another mystery.

'As long as you wear the scabbard,' Merlin warned him, 'you will be safe from harm. Even if you are badly wounded, you will lose no blood. Be sure to wear the scabbard whenever you fight.'

'And what is my destiny?' Arthur asked the old man. 'Look into the future. Shall I be a great king?'

Merlin's eyes grew misty. 'You will become the leader of a band of warriors, the Knights of the Round Table,' he told Arthur. 'You will marry a beautiful queen and build a fine castle. But there is a witch, Morgan le Fay, who has sworn to be revenged on you. She will seek to work her spells to bring about your doom and death. I shall leave you, for I must leave the world of men, and shall journey in the land of ghosts. Throughout your life take care! Keep watch for Morgan le Fay, and never let your sword, Excalibur, be far from you.'

And as King Arthur was to discover, the hatred and enmity of Morgan le Fay were to pursue him throughout his life.

Tristan and the Dragon

Long ago Mark, the King of Cornwall, lived in a castle at Tintagel, perched on the rocky coast of his kingdom. Tristan was the son of the King's sister. She had died shortly after Tristan was born, and, like so many heroes, Tristan grew up in a humble home, not knowing he was a queen's son. By the time that he came to the court of King Mark, Tristan had learned how to fight with bow, lance, sword and dagger, how to leap from trees and other high places without hurt, how to hunt deer silently in the forest and how to sing and play the harp.

One day, when Tristan returned from hunting, he saw that King Mark's face was as dark as a storm-cloud.

'What troubles you?' he asked the King.

'Fifteen years ago I fought a war against the King of Ireland,' said Mark, 'and lost it to his knights. As a punishment, each year I have to pay to the King a rich cargo of gold, corn and fine swords.'

'Refuse all demands!' retorted Tristan. 'It is too great a burden.'

'I cannot refuse,' replied King Mark. 'Come with me and see the champion that the King of Ireland has sent against us.'

A hundred knights stood in the great hall of Tintagel. At one table sat the Irish champion, a huge man, over seven feet tall.

'My name is Morholt!' shouted the champion, and the echo of his great voice rolled like thunder.

'No man dares to stand against Morholt. All Ireland fears me. Who, therefore, will be the challenger, the man that will fight for the King of Cornwall?'

The barons hated this taunting, bullying stranger, but no one dared to speak.

'Lord King,' cried Tristan, 'I will do battle.'

It was decided that the two knights would fight their battle on an island not far from the shore. They would fight alone with none to watch their struggles. They crossed to the island separately in small boats. As they jumped ashore, Tristan pushed his boat adrift.

'One of us only will return,' Tristan said, 'and one boat will be enough.'

From the island the clash of swords, the ringing noise of steel against armour was heard by King Mark and the knights. Hundreds of people lined the shore, waiting to see who would return. All day the battle raged, until, as the sun was setting, the Irish champion's boat came into sight.

'Morholt is the victor,' said the King in deep gloom.

But from the boat stepped Tristan, a broken sword in his hand.

'My lords of Cornwall and of Ireland,' Tristan cried. 'Morholt fought bravely. But my sword pierced his head. It broke in the fight. Here! Take it, Cornwall's gift to Ireland!'

Tristan was received with great joy at the castle of Tintagel. But when the Irish lords returned to their own country, all of Ireland was sad. Morholt had seemed a terrible, cruel man to the Cornishmen, but in his own country he had been a gentle and kind giant. His young niece

Iseult the Fair, a beautiful princess, promised that one day she would gain revenge on the knight who had killed Morholt.

In Tintagel Tristan fell ill. He lay on his couch, white and weak. No medicines could cure him, although doctors came from all parts of the kingdom. No one knew that Morholt's sword had been poisoned. Each day the stench from Tristan's wound increased, until no one could bear to come near him.

'I shall die,' he said, 'but it will be at sea, not here in this bed.' He asked King Mark to put him in a boat with no sail, no oars and no sword in his hand. Mark believed that Tristan was dying and would shortly join the gods, so he prepared the boat as the knight asked.

The little ship drifted away from the shore of Cornwall. Caught by the winds and the tides, it moved north, near to the coast of Ireland. Tristan had taken only one precious possession with him – his harp. He picked it up and played a mournful tune. Fishermen heard his playing but when they reached the boat, all was silent, and Tristan's lifeless hand trailed through the water.

They carried him ashore to the castle of White Haven, where Iseult lived. She had magic medicines which could make people well again. She bathed and dressed Tristan's wound, although she did not know that this was the knight that she had vowed to kill in revenge for the death of Morholt. After a few days the wound was healed, and Tristan could walk along the walls of the castle, wishing himself back to the court at Tintagel.

He waited until he was strong and then one day slipped away, saying not a word to Iseult or to any of the Irish folk. He found his boat and, now playing a joyful tune on his harp, let the breeze carry him to Cornwall. King Mark welcomed him home with great joy, and in Tristan's honour a big feast was held. As for Iseult, when she found that he had gone, she vowed that the next time they met, Tristan would not escape her.

King Mark did not have a wife. Every day his barons asked him to find a princess and marry her, for they thought that if the King did not have sons Cornwall would one day be ruled by Tristan. And they all feared the knight. One morning two swallows sent by Iseult flew by King Mark's window. They dropped from their beaks a lock of woman's hair. It shone like spun gold in the sunlight. King Mark picked it up.

'I will take a wife,' he said, 'and it shall be the Lady with the Hair of Gold. Whoever finds the Lady will receive a great reward.'

When Tristan saw the lock of hair, he recognized immediately that it came from the head of Iseult.

'King Mark,' he said, 'your lords may search the whole world but they will not find the Lady with the Hair of Gold. But I will set my life at peril for you, for the search will mean great danger. I take an oath to die or to bring back the princess who has golden hair to be your wife.'

Tristan fitted out a ship and took a hundred knights with him on the journey. He disguised them and himself as merchants and sailed directly to White Haven. He went ashore alone and was told that Iseult had shut herself away in the castle. She sent out a swallow every day to fly to all parts of the earth in a search for the vanished prince who played the harp.

On the next day the Cornishman heard a great roaring noise, as if a huge brute was in pain. Tristan asked a woman hurrying by the reason for the noise.

'It is a dragon,' she told him, 'the most terrible dragon on earth. Every day it comes to the gates of the city, and every day a maiden has to be given to it. Not all of Iseult's magic can overpower such a dragon. Twenty knights have fought it, and twenty knights lie dead.'

'Can no man kill this dragon?' Tristan asked.

'We wait for such a man,' the woman replied. 'The King of Ireland is in despair. The one man who would have conquered the monster lies dead. Morholt, our champion, was killed by magic in Cornwall.'

'This fight is not for us,' Tristan muttered to his men.

'One other thing,' the old woman went on. 'The King of Ireland has promised the hand of his daughter Iseult in marriage to the knight who kills the beast.'

Tristan returned to his ship and armed himself for the battle. He rode out into open country to seek the dragon. As the monster grew near, Tristan saw that it had the head of a bear, with red eyes like coals of fire, the claws of a lion and the tail of a serpent.

Tristan charged his horse at the dragon with such force that his lance broke into a hundred pieces. He drew his sword and struck the monster's head. Not even the skin was broken. But the beast felt the blow and angrily prepared to burn the prince with a single fiery breath. It charged at the knight, who put up his shield to ward off the flames of fire. The dragon knocked the shield from Tristan's hand with such force that it broke into a hundred pieces. Another

snort of flame from its nostrils burnt his horse to a cinder. Without hesitation, knowing now that he had only one chance of success, Tristan ran close to the dragon and, as its open mouth searched for him, he thrust his sword down the monster's long throat and into its heart. The dragon fell dead. Tristan cut out its tongue and placed it in his belt. But the dragon's poison had touched Tristan's hand, and he fell down in a faint.

As he lay senseless in the bushes, Iseult rode

by. She saw the dead dragon and the knight lying on the ground. His hat had fallen from his head, and she recognized him as the prince with the harp, the man she had sworn to kill. Again she would bring him back from the dead, but only to take her revenge. She touched the poisoned spot with a magic balm and lifted Tristan's sword high over her head.

'Die!' she cried out. 'Die, Tristan, who killed Morholt!'

Tristan awoke from his faint to see the avenger standing over him. 'You have saved me twice from death,' Tristan whispered. 'Now make it three times. Ever since the swallows brought your hair of gold to Cornwall I have searched the oceans for you.'

And Iseult believed him. But when Tristan came to the palace of the King of Ireland, he told a different story.

'I have been sent by King Mark,' he told the Irish chieftain. 'He sends you peace and goodwill and wishes our lands never to be at war. The King's greatest wish is to marry Iseult. All Cornwall will be hers as Queen, and as for you, King of Ireland, you will know then that your enemy is in your power.'

The King therefore agreed to Iseult's marriage to King Mark. And so, by a trick, Tristan was allowed to sail from Ireland with the weeping princess. But on the voyage to Cornwall Tristan came to realize that he loved Iseult. He could bear it no longer, and the night before they reached the Cornish coast he told her of his love.

Iseult wept and told him that although she had sworn to avenge Morholt she could not harm Tristan for she loved him. But she would not go against her father's wishes. And so, at the castle of Tintagel, the wedding of King Mark and Iseult was celebrated with feasting and songs, but there were two sad people at that wedding. Nor does the story end there, for many strange and tragic adventures were to happen to Tristan and Iseult, adventures that were to end in bitter tears and their deaths many years later. But that is another tale.

Volund the Smith

Deep in Lapland, the country of snow and ice, three brothers lived together. One of the brothers, Eghill the Archer, could shoot an arrow a great distance and he hunted for their food. Slagfid the Ironbeater made their swords, shields and tools. Volund the Smith fashioned beautiful gold and silver rings and brooches and made cups and plates.

But the three brothers were not happy. They each wanted a wife to share their life in the forest and by the lake. One morning they saw three maidens sitting by the side of the lake. They were weaving linen coats, and beside them lay three feather coats. The brothers stood amazed, for they recognized the swan maidens who carried the dead from the battlefields to Valhalla, the last resting-place of heroes. The swan maidens were tired of their work and wanted to rest. They had come to Wolfdale to put aside their swan coats for a time and were busily making themselves new summer coats of linen.

The brothers begged them to stay. The three maidens agreed and put away the flying coats made of swan feathers into a chest which the brothers locked. They said they would marry the brothers and never fly again. And so the three men and their wives lived happily in the wooden house by the shores of the lake. Seven years passed. They were happy years, but at the end of the seventh year the maidens grew restless. They had tired of the peaceful life in the forest: they longed to fly again over the trees, to seek for battlefields where men died and to carry their souls to the magic land of Valhalla. The

maidens had been born for this work and knew that they had to return to it.

One day, after the three brothers had gone hunting, the maidens broke open the chest and took out their white swan coats. They decided to try them on again to see if they fitted. At once a great longing came over them. They threw off the linen clothes, flapped their wings and rose high into the sky. Turning south, they soared away, became tiny specks against the blue sky and finally disappeared.

When the brothers returned, they found the house empty.

'They will return before dark,' said Slagfid.

But as darkness fell they became more and more worried. Then Volund noticed that the clothes chest was open. Throwing back the lid, he saw that the white feather coats had gone.

'Will they ever return?' Volund asked his brothers in despair.

'Of course! In a day or two, in a week, they will be with us again,' Eghill said, hopefully.

But a month passed, then two months, then six months. The brothers began to lose hope. They did not hunt or fish; the smithy was cold; the forge was unused. They sat around the lake, watching the sky until daylight faded and the moon mocked them.

'I cannot rest!' shouted Eghill. 'This house is hateful to me. I must leave and search the world until I find my wife.'

And so two of them left Wolfdale. Slagfid went south, and Eghill went east. But Volund stayed at home, hoping that one day his wife would come flying over the tall trees to their forest home.

Lonely and unhappy, Volund went back to his smithy. He spent all his time there, working day and night in the warm, rosy light thrown out by the fire. He began to fashion rings of pure gold set with precious jewels. He had never made such beautiful rings: although he did not know it, he was the finest smith in the whole of the North. He threaded the gold rings on to cords and hung them from the rafters, the windows and the roof. He hoped that if his wife flew over Wolfdale she would see the glittering rings or hear their musical chiming and would be tempted to come down to earth. Soon, hundreds of the rings, tinkling like tiny bells, covered the house both inside and out. By running his fingers along the cords and wires Volund could play different tunes and melodies that brought the animals out of the forest to listen. Even the fierce bears and wolves paused as they passed the golden house.

Wolfdale was in a land ruled by King Nithud. News reached him of the treasure that Volund had made. He came one day to the forest home and, seeing that the smith was fishing in the lake, he crept unnoticed into the house. His greedy eyes widened and glinted at the sight of so much treasure. He could not resist stretching out a hand to take a ring. He slipped away into the trees, hiding there until Volund returned. He sent one of his soldiers to bring the Queen to Wolfdale to see the wondrous house of golden rings.

When Volund returned, he sat down by the fire to cook his meal. As his eyes followed the dancing golden rings, he saw immediately that one was missing. He ran to the door of the smithy, calling out the name of his wife, thinking that she had returned and had taken a ring.

'Hervor! Hervor!' he called, but his words echoed unanswered through the birch trees. He ran to the chest and lifted the lid. There was no feather coat, only the linen dress that Hervor had left. Tired and sad, Volund threw himself down on to his bed of furs and fell into a deep sleep.

He woke suddenly, feeling a terrible weight on his legs and chest. Had the house fallen on him? Had the gods come down to seize him? Then he heard the laughter of his enemy, King Nithud. He struggled to rise from his bed but found that his legs, arms and wrists were weighed down with chains.

'Your own chains bind you,' sneered Nithud. 'Did you not know that I am King and Lord of Wolfdale? All this treasure is mine by right.'

When the Queen entered the forest home, her eyes grew huge at the sight of the jewels and gold rings. A cruel woman, who had long hated Volund and his brothers, the Queen's eyes gleamed at the sight of him in chains.

'Now that you have Volund in your power,' she told her husband, 'cripple him! Make certain that he will never walk again, that you will never have to fear him.'

'How can I do it?' Nithud asked.

'Take your knife and cut the sinews behind his knees.'

King Nithud, as evil as his wife, did as she suggested. The chains were taken from Volund, but he could no longer walk. Maimed, he could only drag himself along the ground, catching at tables and chairs to pull himself forward.

Nithud seized all the treasure, placed Volund's jewelled sword in his belt and gave the two most beautiful rings to the Queen and to his daughter Bothvild. Volund was carried to an island in the sea, his smithy was set up there, and he was forced to work for the King. He fashioned brooches, rings, cups and other precious articles.

Nithud was afraid that someone would find and steal the jewels, so he left the treasure on the island. Not even his wife or his daughter, who begged to go, were allowed to visit the desolate spot pounded by the cold seas.

Volund worked at his forge, silent and full of hate. The King's guards left food on the beach.

He dragged himself down to collect it. No one spoke to him: he spoke to no one. He waited, knowing that one day fate would let him take a terrible revenge on Nithud.

King Nithud had two sons. As they grew up, they heard mysterious stories about the smith who lived on the island. They stole a boat and, telling no one, rowed out to the island. Volund watched them coming. For the first time in years he smiled and spoke.

'Welcome, King's sons,' he told them. 'My humble smithy is yours to explore.'

He showed them his daggers and swords, his anvil and hammers and the great leaping fire.

When Nithud's sons saw the gold and jewels, their eyes glistened with greed.

'Look into this great chest,' invited Volund, and he plunged his arms to the elbows in gold brooches, cups, knives and helmets.

'I would give you these treasures, but the King will take them all from you. Come again tomorrow with a sack and you may take away these fine things and hide them where you will.'

Volund worked all night. He filed the edge of the chest until the lid was as sharp as any knife. Next day the brothers returned.

'Quickly, smith!' they cried. 'Show us the treasures that we are to carry away and hide.'

Volund led them to the chest. Lifting the lid, he made a signal for them to look inside. The boys placed their necks on the edge and gazed greedily at the golden hoard.

'Look closely, my wolf cubs,' Volund suggested. And as they stood there, their throats resting gently on the edge, the smith slammed the sharpened lid down. With their mouths still open, the boys' heads rolled into the chest, and the lifeless bodies fell to the floor.

Volund burned their bodies in a fire so that flesh, bone, hair and clothes all disappeared. He kept only their skulls which he coated with gold and silver and fashioned into drinking cups for King Nithud. From the boys' teeth and eyeballs he made brooches for the Queen and her daughter Bothvild to wear on their gowns.

Nithud sent men to search throughout his kingdom for his sons. He mourned deeply when they could not be found and blamed robbers or wolves for carrying them away. When Volund sent the drinking cups and brooches, the King, his wife and daughter were pleased and for a moment forgot their grief. Princess Bothvild liked her brooch so much that she decided to ask Volund to make a ring to match. She crossed the island and spoke to the smith.

'No one knows that I am here,' she said.

'I will not tell,' Volund replied, 'but I have something more precious than a ring and a brooch.'

'What is it?' Bothvild asked.

He placed before her a coat of silver, so delicate that it seemed to be made of the finest threads.

'I would give anything I possessed for so fine a coat,' she told him.

Volund put the coat into the chest and lifted the lid high.

'Look in and see its changing colours,' said the smith.

But as the princess placed her neck on the edge, Volund saw how young and innocent she was. He could not kill her. Instead, he sent her away, back to her evil father.

Now the time had come to leave the island. Into the silver coat he threaded wild swan's feathers. Drawing the coat about him, he used it as wings to fly into the air. He flew over Nithud's palace. The King and his wife were in the palace yard, their eyes raised to watch him.

'Where are our sons?' they shouted to the smith.

'Their skulls are your cups. Their eyes and teeth hang about your necks. The rest is ashes,' Volund replied.

'A curse on your greed!' cried the Queen to her husband.

'A curse on your cruelty!' cried the King to his wife.

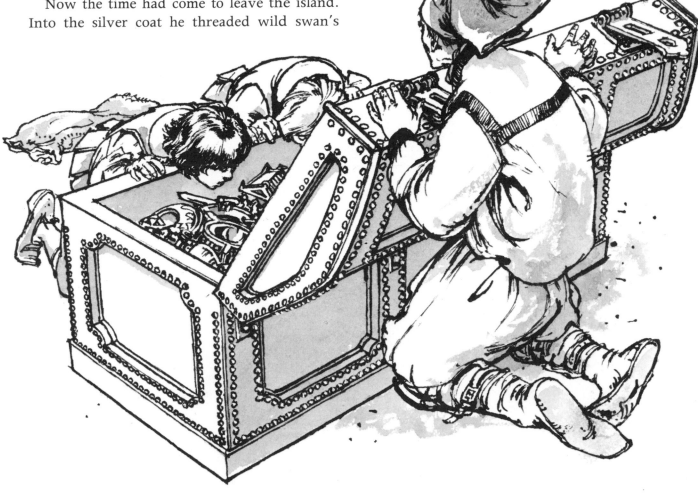

Swiftly, Volund flew higher on his swan's wings. Archers fired arrows at him, but they fell harmlessly away. Higher and higher he climbed. Away in the distance he could see the mountains, rivers and seas of the south. His rage and bitterness left him: a new life lay ahead. Somewhere he would find his two brothers Eghill and Slagfid; at some time he would join his wife Hervor. For the first time in years Volund laughed. He let the warm wind carry him away, gliding towards new adventures in the lands that lay beyond the sea.

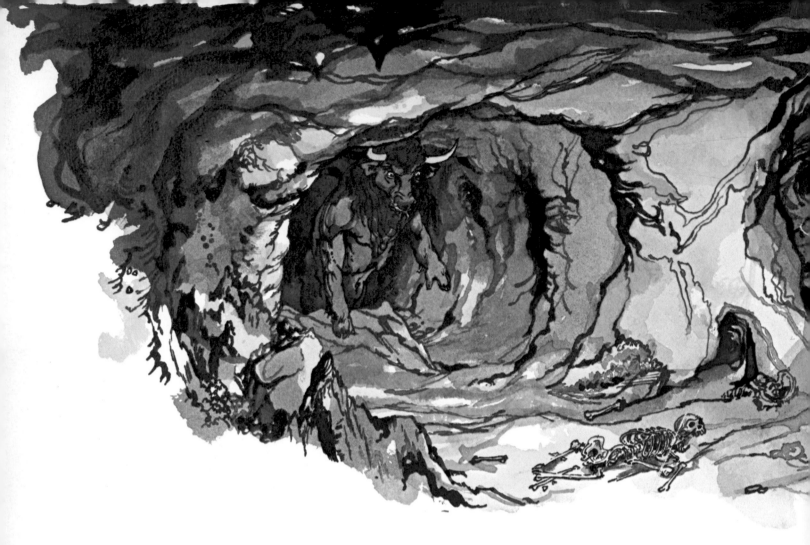

Theseus and the Minotaur

Greece is a country of mountains and forests, baked by a hot sun, cooled by the blue sea. Long ago in the famous city of Athens there lived an old king called Aegeus. He had one son, Theseus, who spent his boyhood with his mother in the distant mountains. Theseus set out for Athens one day and along the road he had many adventures. But there is no time to tell all of these stories.

Shortly after Theseus had arrived in Athens and had taken his place next to the King, his father, he heard one morning a loud wailing noise, the sound of a thousand people crying and screaming. He searched for his father and found him surrounded by a tearful crowd of people.

'What is it? Is there a sickness in Athens? Or an earthquake?' Theseus asked.

'No, my son,' said Aegeus. 'It is the day when

the whole city draws lots to see which seven young men and seven maidens leave Athens to be eaten by the Minotaur.'

'The Minotaur! What is that?'

'The most dangerous and cruel monster in the whole world,' his father told him. 'It lives on the island of Crete, deep underground in a maze of tunnels and passages called the Labyrinth.'

'And what kind of monster is it – a snake or a dragon or a giant?'

Aegeus shook his grey head. 'It is half man, half bull,' he went on, 'with a man's cunning brain and a wild bull's strength.'

'And why should Athens be in fear of it,' asked Theseus, 'if the monster lives miles across the sea?'

His father then told the sad story. He had led the people of Athens into a war with Crete. King Minos, his enemy, had won the war, and when the people of Athens had begged for peace, the King of Crete had insisted that each year seven youths and seven maidens should be sent to feed the Minotaur. And now the terrible day had come again. Everyone feared that their son or their daughter would be chosen.

'Let the people of Athens draw lots for only six young men,' declared the brave Theseus, 'for I will be the seventh. But I will take my sword with the golden handle and I will fight and kill the Minotaur.'

Aegeus wept openly because he thought that Theseus had no chance against the monster. He begged him to stay.

'You are a prince,' he said. 'You do not have to be sacrificed.'

But Theseus would not listen. A ship was prepared, rigged with black sails, and Theseus and his companions went on board. The poor old king and thousands of folk went down to the harbour to see them off.

'My son,' said Aegeus, 'I shall watch from the clifftop every day, waiting for your return. The sails of your ship are black. If you kill or escape from the Minotaur and return to Greece, take down the black sails and hoist white ones so that I shall know that you live. We can then prepare a great feast for your return.'

Theseus promised, and the vessel left Athens' harbour. A breeze carried them to Crete, but as they neared the island and the blue mountains became clearer every day, the more unhappy they became. No one relished the thought of becoming the Minotaur's dinner.

As they approached the island, Theseus saw a flash of light, as if the sun had glinted on metal.

'It is Talus,' the master of the ship told them, 'a giant made entirely of brass.'

As they sailed closer, the giant followed them along the shore, stepping from cliff to cliff, waving an enormous brass club above his head.

'He will drive his club through the deck of the ship,' Theseus said, and put his hand to his sword.

As they came nearer to the harbour, the giant straddled the entrance, with a foot on each clifftop. Then the brass lips opened, and the giant spoke.

'From where come you, strangers?'

Theseus clapped his hands to his ears, for it was as if a hundred church bells had boomed out a message.

'From Athens!' shouted the ship's captain. 'With a cargo for the Minotaur.'

'Pass!' chimed Talus. And he set off again, striding from hill to hill, cliff to cliff, round and round the island. He circled it three times a day on a never-ending journey.

When they landed, the palace guards took the Greeks to King Minos. He was a cruel king. His guardian giant was the Man of Brass, but it was said that King Minos had a heart of iron. He poked the Athenian youths and maidens to make sure that they were plump enough to make a tasty meal for the Minotaur. They all cried quite openly except the brave Theseus. But King Minos did not think that the Greek prince was brave, only insolent.

'Are you not afraid?' the King sneered. 'For this is your last day on earth.'

'I fear no one, not even your monster,' said Theseus, 'and it is you who should be frightened. Do you not look in your mirror? If you did, you would see a monster more horrible than the Minotaur.'

Minos went red with anger, then purple and other colours.

'You will be the first to go,' he told Theseus. 'The monster will have you for his breakfast.'

The angry argument between the two men was watched by Ariadne, the daughter of King Minos. She sat on a throne beside her father and she thought that she had never seen anyone as handsome as the Greek prince. She was a beautiful and tender-hearted girl, quite unlike her cruel father. She wept for the Athenians and, as the guards were taking the Greek away, she fell at her father's feet and begged him to set them all free. And she had a special word for their young and fearless leader.

'Do not concern yourself with these affairs of state,' Minos replied, 'and be thankful that there are Greeks for the Minotaur to eat. He has a great appetite, and if there were no Greeks, your own people would be served up like fat chickens for his supper.'

The seven youths and seven maidens were then put in a prison. The guard told Theseus to get some sleep because the Minotaur preferred an early breakfast. But Theseus kept awake and paced the floor of the prison.

Just before midnight the door opened, and Ariadne appeared before him.

'Prince Theseus,' she whispered, 'are you awake?'

She led him from the dungeon into the bright moonlight.

'Go to your ship,' she told him, 'and sail quickly to your homeland.'

'I want my sword, not my ship,' said the prince. 'I will never leave Crete until I have fought the Minotaur and delivered Athens from this cruel law.'

She gave him his sword and led him by the hand through the woods, until they came to a high wall, smooth and unbroken. Ariadne pressed her finger against a block of stone which swung open to show a dark tunnel leading into the hillside. The door closed silently behind them.

55

'This is the Labyrinth,' said Ariadne, 'a maze of paths through the rock. If you left the door-way, you could wander through the tunnels for a lifetime and never find your way out.'

Just then Theseus heard the echo of a roar, a sound that grew in strength as it rumbled through the passageways. He shivered, but more with fear than with cold.

'That is the Minotaur,' whispered Ariadne. 'He lives in a cave at the centre of the maze. Follow the sound and you will find the monster.'

'How will I return?' asked Theseus.

'Take one end of this silken string,' the princess told him, 'and I shall hold tightly to the other end. If you defeat the Minotaur, the string will guide you to me.'

Theseus set off, unwinding the silken cord as he stumbled along. There were doors, and steps, and tunnels that seemed to go in a circle, and crooked passageways. As he passed through, the noise of the monster grew louder, like a bull's roaring but with the sound of a human voice in it. Then, when he felt that his ear-drums would burst, Theseus suddenly entered the cave. The Minotaur stood before him. The great horns were lowered as if to charge at the prince. Instead of four legs, the Minotaur stood erect like a man on two powerful hind legs. The creature spoke in a kind of half-human, strangled voice. Theseus shivered again, for he could not make out the words, but the message was clear.

He dodged the first charge, and the bull broke a horn as it crashed into the wall of the cave. It roared so loudly with pain that part of the Labyrinth fell down. The people of Crete thought that an earthquake had rocked the island.

On the second charge the Minotaur grazed Theseus' side, knocking the prince to the ground. The monster then opened its great mouth to snap off Theseus' head with one gulp. But at this moment Theseus leaped from the ground and with his sword sliced off the Minotaur's head with one blow.

Again the earth rumbled and shook. Perhaps this really was an earthquake? He felt a tug on the silken string and ran swiftly through the tunnels towards the entrance. Ariadne was waiting.

'The city is collapsing,' she said. 'We must run to the ship.'

They went first to the prison and released the other Greeks. Then they ran to the harbour as the shrieks of the Cretans mixed with the noise of falling houses. The earthquake, if that is what it was, continued to rock the city. They saw Minos' palace slowly crumble into dust.

As their ship turned towards the mouth of the harbour, they saw the flashing figure of Talus, the Man of Brass, come striding along the cliff-tops. He swung his club as if driven by clock-work. The little ship had reached open sea by the time that Talus straddled the cliffs. He lifted his club above his head, overbalanced and fell face forward into the sea, sinking quickly, carried to the fishes by his great weight.

Ariadne looked back sadly at the land of Crete. She did not want to leave her father, but her love for Theseus was so great that she would go anywhere with him. And so the ship with the black sail left Crete, carrying Ariadne and Theseus to more adventures across the sea.

But this story did not have a happy ending. On the journey home Theseus landed on an island where he and Ariadne stayed for some months. Then Theseus grew tired of her. One day he slipped away, boarded his ship and sailed off. Ariadne stood sadly on the shore watching the black sail as it became smaller and smaller in the distance.

In return the gods played a trick on cruel Theseus. In his excitement to be home he forgot to change the sail. Aegeus, his father, who had kept watch every day, saw the ship of his son Theseus approaching. The sail was black. In his grief he threw himself from the cliff to die on the sharp rocks below. And so, when Theseus came home, instead of songs and laughter he was met with weeping and wailing.

Horatius at the Bridge

Horatius was a soldier in the Roman army, a captain in charge of the garrison that guarded one of the gates into the city. On one side of Rome was the fast-flowing river Tiber; on the other three sides the people had built high walls to protect themselves against their enemies. And at that time Rome had many enemies. These were the days before powerful Roman legions crossed mountains, rivers and seas to conquer lands in Germany, Britain and Africa. Horatius lived in the city when it was weak and small, when strong neighbouring rulers thought that they would march in and capture it for themselves.

One of these enemies was Porsena, King of Clusium, a nearby city. News came to him that Roman soldiers had crossed into his land. Here was the chance he had been waiting for.

'Send out messengers to all parts of Clusium and to the lands and cities beyond,' he ordered. 'Summon an army to our flag! These proud Romans will feel the edges of our swords!'

Soldiers rode to all parts of Italy. Horsemen, foot-soldiers, archers, princes and peasants all flocked to join King Porsena. The Romans had many enemies, and every one of them hoped that the city would fall and that they could steal or destroy one part of Rome.

Sitting on his white horse, his golden cloak pulled tightly around him, the King watched ten thousand horsemen ride past, the red and yellow plumes on their silver helmets dancing and bobbing as they rode by. For another hour he sat on his patient horse while an even greater horde of marching soldiers saluted him.

News reached Rome that a great army was preparing to march. The walls of the city were strengthened; farmers and their families from nearby villages poured across the Tiber bridge; every man and boy was given a sword.

Horatius and his small band of soldiers took guard at the gate over the bridge. One man climbed to the pinnacle of the gate to look out over the green countryside.

'They come! They come!' he shouted, and raised his arm to point to the distant hills. Black smoke poured skywards, and the flash of the sun on armour seemed like the reflection of a thousand mirrors. When darkness came, the red flames of blazing villages lit up the midnight sky. News came that one after another the farms and the outposts of Rome had fallen to Porsena's army. Every guardpost, every signal station was in the hands of the invaders.

At daylight next morning the Commander of the city garrison inspected the defences.

'We have very little time,' he said. 'Only the river Tiber and the city walls now lie between us and the spears of the Etruscan soldiers.'

'What of the bridge?' asked one of his captains. 'For the Etruscans will pour across it and into the heart of our city.'

'The bridge must come down!' the Commander ordered. 'Bring axes and start the work at once.'

Then, suddenly, a rider raced through the fields, his eyes wide with fear.

'To arms!' he shouted, falling on his knees. 'Porsena and his army are upon us!'

The Commander looked towards the hills. Only two or three miles away a red dust-cloud was moving slowly along the road, and behind it stretched a mass of marching men, advancing towards the city.

'They are foxes, those Etruscans,' cried the Commander, 'for they have used the darkness to hide them. And if we do not break down the bridge, we shall be their chickens.'

The dust-cloud edged nearer. 'They will soon be upon us,' said the Commander, 'before the bridge goes down. And if they win the crossing, the whole of Rome is at their mercy.'

Horatius had been watching and listening. He now stepped forward.

'I am the Captain of the gate,' he told the Commander, 'and, as you can see, it is a narrow place. Three men can defend this bridge. I and two of my bravest soldiers will stand guard at the gate while your axes fly. A thousand men can be stopped by three!'

Immediately, two men came forward.

'I will stand at your right hand,' said Lartius.

'And I will guard your left hand,' echoed Herminius.

Armed with sword and spear and with dag-

58

gers in their belts, the three men took their places at the end of the bridge. Behind them they heard the noise of axes as they rose and fell against the timbers of the bridge. But the sound was lost in the roar of hooves and the crash of armour as King Porsena approached at the head of his army. A sea of gold and silver dazzled the Romans: four hundred trumpets bellowed out the Etruscan war salute; spears and armour caught the sun and flung the glare into the eyes of the citizens as they watched from the river bank and from behind the city's walls. It was a fearsome sight.

A shout of laughter went up from the Etruscan army when they saw three men standing against them. Elbowing others aside, three princes in Porsena's army stepped forward. Together they ran to the bridge, their long spears held out before them. Lartius turned one prince and flung him into the racing river. Herminius drove his sword between the teeth of the second prince, and Horatius went down on one knee to thrust his sword into the third man. One after another the Etruscan heroes came forward to challenge the Romans. Each one in turn fell into the blood-stained dust or the foaming river. The waving spears, the sea of steel wavered.

The King rallied his men. 'Forward, forward!' he cried. 'One more rush will succeed. We can sweep them aside for they are brave but weary men.'

But the axes had done their work. The pillars of the bridge had been cut through, all but the last strands. The bridge lurched, ready to fall into the Tiber.

'Come back! Come back!' shouted the Commander. And all the people echoed him.

apart, as if in fury or as a sign of what would happen if any man dared to fall or jump into the raging torrent.

Horatius stood alone on the bank. Behind him was the dangerous river; in front stood thirty thousand men.

'Yield to us! Surrender, for you are a brave Roman but now you stand alone,' said King Porsena.

Horatius was silent. He glanced back over his shoulder. Across the river, on a hillside, stood his house. He could see quite clearly the white porch and the dark green of the trees where his sons played their games as Roman soldiers. He slid his bloody sword into its sheath and turned towards the river.

'Father Tiber,' he cried, 'all Rome prays to you to save our city. Take me today. Or save me. Such be your will!' And he plunged into the water which closed over his head.

Two armies watched the river. No one spoke. Then, breaking the surface, they saw the crest of Horatius' helmet. The Romans cheered, and even some of the Etruscan soldiers shouted, urging Horatius to strike out for the opposite bank. But his armour was heavy and pulled him down. Twice he sank below the surface, and twice he rose again. The third time that he went down Horatius felt the bed of the river beneath his feet and he pushed himself ashore.

A crowd ran to the water's edge, lifted him high on their shoulders and carried him into the city.

'Your hands are washed clean of Etruscan blood,' said the Commander, 'but Rome will never forget that you saved the city. Choose any reward you wish, and it will be granted.'

'Give me two oxen and corn land,' said Horatius, 'for that is all I want from Rome.'

So he returned to his home, and when the Etruscans left and the city was safe, he took the plough to his field and became a farmer, happy to work the land until Rome should need him again.

'Back, Lartius! Back, Herminius! Back, Horatius!' cried a thousand voices.

First Lartius ran across the shaking bridge. Then Herminius crossed. As they passed, beneath their feet the timbers groaned and cracked. But before Horatius could leave his post the beams broke and fell into the torrent. The river picked up the broken timbers and smashed them

Black Colin of Loch Awe

Among the great families of Scotland the clan Campbell was one of the most feared. The chief of the clan lived in a castle on the shores of Loch Awe. Behind the castle rose the wild mountain of Ben Cruachan. This mountain gave the Campbells their battle cry of 'Cruachan' which over many years had terrified the enemies of the clan.

The son of the chief was called Colin. In those days a chief's son, when still a boy, lived with one of the families in the clan for several years. He would thus learn how the poorer people lived. As he grew up, Colin showed himself to be a real leader. He could beat the other boys at wrestling, running, swimming in the cold loch and in hunting the wild deer. He was quickest with the dirk (a Scottish dagger) and with the two-edged sword, the claymore. When other clans rode down to Loch Awe to steal sheep and cattle, young Colin joined the Campbells. He became known as Black Colin. Was this because of his black hair and beard, or because of his fierceness against his enemies? No one knew, but Black Colin was feared throughout the glens.

The old chief died, and Colin became the leader of the Campbells. He married a beautiful young woman from another clan who was known as the Lady of Glenurchy. But Colin had one great enemy. In the next glen lived Neil MacCorquodale. He envied Black Colin's lands and power and above all hated Colin for marrying the Lady of Glenurchy. Neil waited, hoping that one day he would be able to strike down his enemy and seize his wife.

One day news came to Scotland of the great crusade that was to set out for the Holy Land of Palestine. The Turks had killed many Christians on the road to Jerusalem and the Holy Places. The Pope in Rome had called on all Christian fighting men to go on crusade, to win back the city of Jerusalem and the places where Christ had once walked.

Colin was restless in Loch Awe. He knew the mountains; every day for years he had hunted wild boar; no man dared to raise his hand against the Campbells. Colin wanted fresh excitement. He decided to go on the crusade, to fight in the Christian army against the Turks. He chose ten of his best fighting men to go with him. The rest would stay behind to guard his castle, his lands and his wife. The Lady of Glenurchy pleaded with Colin to stay. But the chief had grown tired of the mists of Scotland. He wanted to travel to the Holy Land to see for himself the wonders of the East.

'You will rule the glen for me,' he told his wife. 'Wait seven years. At the end of this time, if I have not returned, you must take another husband to rule over the lands of Loch Awe.'

'I will wait seven times seven years,' replied the Lady of Glenurchy, 'but I could not find and love a husband as I love you. Give me a token. If you are wounded and near to death, send it to me as a sign. Then I will know that you are dead and will never return to Loch Awe.'

Black Colin ordered a gold ring to be made. On the inside of the ring both their names were marked. He broke the ring in two. One half he gave to his wife, the other he kept himself.

'I will return my half of the ring to you only if I am dying,' he said. 'You will know then that I shall never return.'

Colin then set off on his long journey. He travelled by ship and on horseback through France, crossed the high mountains of the Alps and after many months reached the city of Rome. The Pope sent him to join the famous army of the Knights Templars on the island of Rhodes. From the white-walled castle, bleached by a blazing sun, the Templars sailed for Palestine to fight the Turks. They landed and marched along the road towards Jerusalem. The Templars, dressed in long cloaks to protect them from the sun's burning heat, rode into battle on their fine horses. But the Turks did not stay in the same position. They rode lighter, smaller horses which darted in and out of the ranks of the Templars. Firing from horseback, the Turks handled their bows and arrows with great skill, so that many Christians fell wounded. The Scottish clansmen shouted their war-cry 'Cruachan!' as they charged, but the Turks melted away towards the desert and safety.

The Christians did not give up. They marched on, charging at the Turks whenever they came too near. But the accurate arrows of the enemy and the heat of the sun took its toll. The Scottish clansmen fell one by one, brought down by disease or wounds. Only Black Colin remained, and he and the Templars struggled on until they reached the Sea of Galilee. Here Colin fell ill and lay for many weeks in his tent near to death. Unknown to him, seven years had passed since he had left the shores of Loch Awe.

Deep in the misty mountains of Scotland the Lady of Glenurchy waited. No word had been received from Black Colin: surely he must be dead. Chiefs from other clans began to raid the glen, stealing cattle. Other men came to the castle to ask the Lady to marry them. She sent them all away. She told no one but was determined not to believe that Colin was dead until she received the half-ring.

Neil MacCorquodale was keen to marry her and to join the Glenurchy lands with his own. He tried to trick her by bringing to Loch Awe a man who said that he had travelled from Rome with a letter. She opened it and read that Black Colin had been killed fighting against the Turks.

'Have you anything else for me?' she asked. 'A token or a ring?'

The messenger looked puzzled. But Neil spoke quickly. 'There is no sign or token,' he said. 'The story is that as Colin lay dying he gave a message and a ring to a friend. The message was that his Lady should marry a strong neighbour and so bring peace to the Glenurchy lands. But then the Turks suddenly attacked the camp, captured the precious token and wounded the messenger. He told the story to my friend here who has come from Rome with this sad tale.'

Neil then rode away, leaving the Lady of Glenurchy in tears. She believed the false story and for weeks would speak to no one. She knew in her heart that the glen needed a chieftain to protect the farmers from their enemies. She sent for Neil and said that she would marry him but that the marriage would not take place until a castle had been built in memory of Black Colin. When the last stone of the castle was laid, then she would become the wife of Neil. The work began, the walls of the castle grew higher and higher, but still there was no news of Colin.

One old woman living in the glen still believed that Colin was alive. She and her family had looked after him when he had been a boy. She told her own son, Ian, to travel to Rome to seek out the truth. Ian set off and journeyed across the sea, over the mountains, through forests and past the cities of Europe before he arrived in Rome.

'Go to the island of Rhodes,' he was told, 'for your chief was taken there to recover from wounds and disease. He may be dead. He may be alive.'

Again Ian set out. He found a ship to take him to the island, landed at the steps leading to the castle and saw a lonely figure standing on the battlements, staring out over the sea. The two men came face to face.

'It is a face that I know well,' cried Colin. 'Can it be my clansman Ian? Have you come to fight the Turks?'

Ian quickly told his chief how all the folk of the glen wept for him, thinking that he was dead. He said that after seven years without a sign the Lady of Glenurchy was preparing to marry Neil who had tricked her into believing that Colin was dead.

'She has told the builders to work slowly on the new castle,' Ian went on, 'but if you do not return quickly, she will marry Neil.'

'I have never forgotten Scotland,' Colin said, 'but I felt that I should stay to fight the Turks. Now my work here is over. I have given seven years of my life to the crusade. We will return to Scotland tomorrow.'

But tomorrow became weeks. They found a ship to carry them home, but the journey was long, and strong winds blew them around the oceans. As each day passed, Colin swore to be avenged on Neil MacCorquodale, and Ian knew now how he had earned the title of Black Colin, for his temper was as black as a raven's wing.

They landed on the Scottish coast and hurried to the glen.

'I shall stay in the hills,' said Colin. 'You go down to the town. Find out what has happened and bring me some old and ragged clothes.'

Ian hurried back. 'The wedding is to take place tomorrow,' he cried, 'for the new castle is finished.'

They went first to Ian's house. His old mother was overjoyed to see them.

'Go now to your wife,' she told Colin.

'No,' he replied, 'for there is a law in Scotland that if a man is away for more than seven years his wife is free to marry. I do not know if my wife still loves me. If she does not, she can marry Neil.'

The old woman thought for a while.

'I have a plan,' she said. 'You must do as I say.'

On the next day Colin dressed in the old

clothes and went to the door of his castle. At one end of the great hall sat the Lady of Glenurchy, pale and not smiling, dressed in a wedding gown. Scraps of food were brought out to the beggars, as was the custom. Colin stood among them.

He shouted out, loudly, 'It is said that the bride should bring bread and ale to beggars on her wedding day.'

Hearing him, the Lady stood up and carried the bread and ale to the door. Colin ate and drank. When he had finished, he returned the empty drinking horn to the Lady. He dropped the half-ring inside it. She picked it out of the horn and looked at her husband. Colin was silent. His glance told her that she did not have to speak. He was willing to go away without saying a word, and she was free to marry Neil if she wished.

But the Lady of Glenurchy spoke out in a loud and joyful voice.

'See!' she cried. 'Black Colin stands before us. We will have a feast, sure enough, and not for a new wedding but for an old one. We shall all eat and drink to Colin, Lord of Loch Awe.'

When Neil heard these words, he ran towards his horse, intending to escape. Colin reached for a claymore.

'I have waited many weeks,' Colin called out, 'and now Neil's blood will flow.'

'No!' the Lady of Glenurchy begged. 'Let him remain alive. There should be no killing on this happy day.'

And so Neil was allowed to ride away. He never again set foot in the glen. As for Black Colin and his wife, they went to live in the new castle at Kilchurn and ruled wisely for many years by the shores of Loch Awe.

Roland and the Battle of Roncesvalles

Charlemagne, King of France, ruled over a large and powerful empire. He feared no other kings, for he had been victorious in many battles. But across the border in neighbouring Spain were the Saracens, a fierce and dangerous army of Turks who had conquered north Africa and most of Spain. They had crossed into France, and Charlemagne had needed France's best soldiers to fling them back across the mountain barrier of the Pyrenees.

The Saracens refused to give up. They had their own religion which drove them forward to fight against the Christians, many of whom had been forced to come to terms. Among the Christian kings of Spain who had surrendered to the Turks was Marsilius. He had been defeated many times by the Saracens and in desperation he had agreed to help them against Charlemagne.

The French armies moved into Spain. At Charlemagne's right hand was Roland, a loyal knight, the King's champion, winner of many battles. The French marched into the territory of Marsilius and sent messengers ordering the Spanish king to submit to Charlemagne. News came to Charlemagne as he waited in his tent that Marsilius had begged for peace and would pay tribute in gold and silver to the King of France. Marsilius asked the King to send his most trusted knight to arrange the amount of the tribute.

'Who shall I send?' thought Charlemagne. 'The brave, faithful Roland or scheming, tricky Ganelon who could tempt a wolf away from its kill?' The King called his two knights together. 'Ganelon, you will go to Marsilius,' he said,

'but beware. The King of Spain is as clever with falsehoods as Roland is with a sword. But you will match him, Ganelon, for you are a man with wits as sharp as a dagger blade.'

Ganelon bowed his head, not sure if the King was praising him or doubting him.

'Be on your guard always,' the King went on, 'for Marsilius will seek to deceive you.'

'No man on earth can trick a fox,' boasted Ganelon. 'Before two days have passed Marsilius will have surrendered his whole kingdom to me.'

Ganelon travelled to Saragossa, where he was received with great honour by Marsilius. For days on end there were games, feasts, balls and exhibitions of horsemanship. The ladies in the pavilions threw flowers at Ganelon and the French knights and shouted out their names in triumph. The French soldiers were overcome with admiration for Marsilius and the great honour that he did them.

Marsilius invited Ganelon to sit by him at the side of a pool in the garden of the palace. The two cunning men watched each other's reflected faces in the smooth water of the pool.

'Your ruler, the great soldier Charlemagne, has done me many injuries,' began Marsilius. 'He has invaded my land, torn down fruit trees, burned farms, seized corn to feed his army and has brought great suffering on the people.'

Ganelon retorted that Charlemagne had marched into Spain to fight the Saracens, the enemies of all Christians. And who had given support to these non-believers but the Christian King of Spain?

And so the argument went back and forward until Marsilius suggested something new.

'Is not Roland the favourite of your King?' he asked, innocently.

Ganelon scowled.

'My people say that Charlemagne intends to give Roland lands and castles in Spain as a reward for his services to the King,' Marsilius went on. 'Should you not be this favoured one?'

And so by silver-tongued flattery and talk Marsilius put the seeds of envy into Ganelon's mind.

Finally, the King of Spain asked, 'If Roland was dead, would you not take his place in Charlemagne's favour?'

Ganelon was easily won over. They drew up a plan. Marsilius would pretend to submit and would invite Roland to come to the village of Roncesvalles, which lay between the two armies, to receive the tribute. It would be a great triumph for Roland. But instead of corn and gold the whole of Marsilius' army would wait to receive him.

After the two men had made their plans, Ganelon returned to Charlemagne. He told the King that Marsilius had humbly submitted and was on his way to Roncesvalles to pay tribute. Roland had been named as the knight to receive the surrender. To make sure that he would not be involved in the treachery Ganelon asked permission to return to France. By the time that Roland set off with his band of knights Ganelon was far along the road to France.

Marsilius made his preparations. Secretly he moved three armies into the woods near Roncesvalles. One of these armies was of Saracen soldiers, armed with the two-edged sword, the scimitar, feared by all Christians. Marsilius also set up tables which groaned under the weight of food and wine.

As Roland prepared to ride from Charlemagne's headquarters, Baldwin, son of Ganelon, came up to him.

'Take me with you,' he begged Roland, 'for I wish to share in the glory won by my father and received by you.'

Roland agreed, and Baldwin was among the hundred knights who rode along the road to Roncesvalles.

When the knights reached the village, Roland sent his friend Oliver to a mountaintop. Oliver came thundering down the slope, full of anger and dismay.

'An army is encamped in the valley,' he cried, 'and dressed in full battle armour. This is not the sign of friendship.'

'I suspected it,' said Roland.

'Then we must return to Charlemagne,' Oliver hurried on, 'and escape from this trap.'

'The trap is closed. Our duty now is to find Marsilius. And not to greet him as friend and ally but to kill him as an enemy.' He spurred his horse forward. 'The blood that will be shed in this valley today will be remembered for ever.'

As they descended into the plain, a second army came into view, made up of Saracens, a thousand flags flying boldly in the summer air.

'Now, my friends,' said Roland, 'every man must fight for himself. Every one here is a perfect knight. Fight today as champions of King Charlemagne, and your deeds will be remembered throughout history.'

The little troop of knights stood close together while the great armies watched them. The first charge of the Saracens and their allies crumbled against the rock of the knights. Horses wheeled away out of the battle, their riders hanging lifeless from the saddles. Of the Christians only Oliver, Roland's friend, was wounded. But even he was able to stay upright as the second attack thundered against the Christian troops.

The leader of the Saracen army was King Falseron. He rode out ahead of his soldiers, waving them to be silent.

'Roland!' he called out. 'Do you remember my son? He died by your hand in battle.' Then he turned to his men. 'Let no one place a finger on Roland,' he cried. 'He belongs to myself. The

revenge of my son's death is mine alone.'

He launched his horse in a charge that took him close to Roland. The Christian champion, who had not moved, now dashed at Falseron with a furious swift charge and thrust his lance through the King's body before Falseron could even lift his shield. The King fell lifeless from his horse, and a groan went up as if from one throat from the Saracen army. They would have left the battlefield immediately, had not Marsilius cut off their retreat with his own men.

71

Baldwin killed Saracens with lance and sword until an arrow pierced his armour and he fell dead. Oliver, blinded by his own blood, did not see a sword striking at his heart. Surrounded by only a handful of his knights, Roland raised a hunting horn to his lips and blew three times.

King Charlemagne was sitting with his court at the foot of the valley when the notes of the horn rolled through the mountains.

'Did you hear it?' he asked his nobles. 'What is its meaning?'

No one dared to answer for all knew that it was the sound of a man desperate for help.

'Ride! Ride!' called Charlemagne.

But as the French army slowly began to move towards Roncesvalles, Roland was nearing the end of his long battle. His horse grew weary first, buckled at the knees and rolled over, dead. On his feet Roland struck his sword fiercely against a rock, thinking that the steel blade which had served him well would never fall into the hands of the Saracens. But the rock burst open with the force of the blow while the sword remained unharmed. Then, overcome by his wounds, Roland sank to the ground and died.

As Charlemagne approached the battlefield, he had to turn his eyes away from the horror. The whole valley resembled a slaughterhouse. Blood and dirt mixed beneath their feet, the stench of death rose up all around them, and the groans of the wounded could not be endured. Charlemagne cursed Roncesvalles as a place of death and treachery where grass should never grow again. He vowed to take revenge against Marsilius and the Saracens.

Every man in the King's army hardened his heart and without an order turned to march on Saragossa. Marsilius was captured and was hung from the battlements of his city. Ganelon was seized and brought back to the field of Roncesvalles to be put to death and be buried alongside his son. And, as Roland had said, the battlefield in the valley of Roncesvalles was remembered for ever.

'Learn from the death of Falseron,' shouted Roland, 'and carry the fight to the enemy.' He rode forward. At his right hand was Baldwin, son of Ganelon.

'It is strange,' said Baldwin. 'No man will come against me. I have slain men on my right and on my left, but no Saracen will come near me.'

'Take off your fine coat with its badge,' said Roland contemptuously. 'Your father has sold us to Marsilius, and his son is clearly not to be harmed.'

'If I should escape dying,' answered Baldwin, 'I shall plunge this sword through my father's heart for his villainy. But I am no traitor, and today your enemies are my enemies.'

The battle became very fierce. Twenty of Marsilius' men fell for every one of the Christian knights. But Roland grieved to see his men go down under the hooves of Marsilius' cavalry.

Jason and the Golden Fleece

Trumpeters and heralds travelled to all parts of Greece, inviting heroes to join Jason in his search for the Golden Fleece. Hundreds of men answered the call, and from them Jason chose fifty men for the crew of his ship, the *Argo*, which had seats for that number of rowers.

'What is this Golden Fleece?' asked Hercules, one of the chosen warriors.

'Zeus, King of the Gods, sent a winged ram to earth,' Jason told them. 'It had skin and wool of gold and magic powers. The ram was sacrificed to the gods, and its Golden Fleece was hung in a cave, guarded by a fearsome serpent. My mission is to bring back the Fleece, and you will be my helpers, the fifty greatest heroes that Greece has ever known.'

On the voyage of the *Argo* Jason and his men had many adventures. One day they called at the island of Lemnos for water and food. A few months earlier the women of Lemnos had murdered all their husbands because they had treated the women very cruelly. The women of Lemnos tempted the Argonauts (so called because they sailed in the *Argo*) to stay, and it took all the great strength of Hercules to seize each man and drag him back to the ship.

The *Argo* sailed eastwards, past the city of Troy and into a strange sea. Hercules had brought an orphan boy called Hylas with him. At another island Hylas went ashore to fill a water jug. As he bent over a pool, water nymphs who lived deep in the pool caught his hands and pulled him head first into the water, dragging him down into the depths where he lived with them among the pale fronds and flowers that grew there. Hercules was very angry and blamed the peasants who lived on the island for the disappearance of Hylas. He wanted to kill every one of them, but Jason stopped him. When the *Argo* sailed, Hercules remained behind to continue the search for Hylas. He never found the orphan boy and had to continue his journey by land.

After further adventures, the Argonauts reached Colchis, the land of the Golden Fleece. A strong guard under the command of the King of Colchis prevented the Argonauts from landing.

'Go home, young man, before I cut out your tongue,' threatened the King.

Jason tried to tempt him. 'You must have many enemies, O great King,' he began. 'I and these Greek heroes will conquer all your enemies and their lands, if only you will give us the Golden Fleece as our reward.'

After a great deal of argument, the King told Jason that he could have the Fleece if he per-

formed four very difficult tasks. The King made these tasks so impossible that all the Argonauts spoke of going home immediately.

'First,' said the King of Colchis, 'you are to tame two fire-breathing bulls. Next, you have to harness them to a plough made of stone and plough a four-acre field. Thirdly, you are to sow the field with the teeth of a dragon and kill the men who will grow from the teeth. And lastly, there is a serpent guarding the Fleece that you will have to overcome.'

Jason could not have done these tasks alone. Fortunately for him the King's youngest daughter, Medea, had caught a glimpse of him and had fallen deeply in love. She was a sorceress with magic powers that were soon brought into play. She smeared the juice of a crocus on his body, and the ointment protected him against the flames of the bulls' breath. He fought the beasts and stunned them with blows to their heads. Then he yoked them to the plough and sowed the field. Sure enough, the dragons' teeth that he placed in neat rows turned into fighting men armed with spears. Medea put into Jason's hand a magic stone which he threw into the field. The soldiers turned on each other and fought until every man lay dead.

When the King found that Jason had completed three of the tasks, he was very worried.

'You shall not have the Fleece,' he cried. 'The serpent will kill you. Go home to Greece.'

'My brave Argonauts will not allow me to leave,' Jason boasted, 'for they say that a man who can tame bulls will have no fear of snakes.'

'My daughter Medea helped you unfairly,' the King accused him. 'I command you to leave Colchis before dawn.'

In the darkest night, as Jason lay awake wondering what to do next, Medea came to him. With a finger to her lips, she led him from the palace to the temple where the Golden Fleece hung on its nail. The serpent, its evil head twisting and turning, the poison from its tongue oozing over the steps of the temple, awaited him.

'My father is planning to kill you in the morning!' Medea whispered.

'I fear the snake,' Jason told her.

'My magic spells will overcome it,' Medea promised. She began to sing in a soft, soothing voice, and the serpent's eyes closed in sleep. Swiftly, she sprinkled poppy juice on its eyelids so that they could not be opened. Poison flew everywhere as the serpent hissed in its blind rage. Jason dodged the drops, grasped the Golden

Fleece and ran for the *Argo*. But a sentry had seen him and gave the alarm. The Argonauts had to fight their way out of the harbour and into the open sea. Many were wounded, but Medea, who had joined them, smeared ointment from her box of magic medicines and spells on their wounds and healed them.

'My father, the King, will never forgive you,' warned Medea. 'For you have stolen both the Fleece and his daughter. He will follow you to the ends of the earth.'

Sure enough, as the *Argo* crossed the sea, the King's fleet could be seen in the distance, steadily chasing them. Then a storm blew up and drove the ship into a harbour on the island of Corfu.

Jason asked the King of that land for protection. At suppertime the Admiral of the Colchian fleet also visited the King.

'A rascal called Jason has run off with the King's daughter,' he said. 'We have been sent to take her home and also the Golden Fleece which they have stolen.'

The King of Corfu answered: 'It is late in the day. Return in the morning when my head will be clearer.'

The King then called for Jason to come to the palace. 'If you marry Medea, you can stay on the island. But if you do not, I shall surrender you to King Colchis.'

Jason thought deeply. Medea was a witch, and who wanted to be married to someone who could slap a spell on her husband? But there was also the serpent, waiting for its revenge. Jason did not hesitate for long, and Medea spoke even more urgently.

'Hurry! Hurry!' she called out. 'Let us get married at once!'

Next morning the Admiral was told about the midnight wedding. He did not dare to return to Colchis and sent a messenger instead. When he heard the news of his daughter's marriage to Jason the thief, the King went into a great rage and fell down dead.

The Argonauts set off and were again blown by a strong wind. This time they landed at Crete where a mechanical man made entirely of bronze guarded the harbour. He flung rocks at passing ships and kicked up huge waves. But the Argonauts were safe with Medea on board their ship. She turned her brilliant eyes on the bronze man and bewitched him so that he staggered about the island, struck his heel against a rock and fell head first into the sea.

After many adventures, Jason reached his homeland to find that King Pelias had given orders that he was to be murdered. But Medea had no worries.

'I shall go to the palace,' she said, 'and teach King Pelias some manners.'

She disguised herself as an old woman and pretended to be a kind goddess who held Pelias in great favour.

'I can make you into a young and handsome prince again,' she told the King.

'Do it quickly, old woman, before I grow a day older,' said Pelias.

Medea set to work. She slaughtered an old sheep, cut its body into pieces and boiled them in an iron pot. She added magic herbs and spells to the stew. Then, while the King was looking the other way, Medea pulled a live year-old lamb from the pot. Among her skills, the sorceress was a conjuror.

'See!' she smiled. 'You can be young, too. The same spell will work for a king as it does for an old sheep.'

Pelias, excited, ordered one of his daughters to chop him up with an axe and to boil the pieces in the pot. She did so, but as the pot boiled and gurgled, no young, live king appeared.

Medea laughed. 'Kings like other men can be fools,' she muttered.

Jason came out of his hiding-place and hung the Golden Fleece in a temple dedicated to the god Zeus. He and Medea settled down to live in this land and for a time they were very happy until she again began to work her magic tricks. But that is another story.

El Cid, the Champion

In Spain, hundreds of years ago, a terrible war raged over the countryside. In those days Spain had not one but many Christian kings. They ruled in the mountains where they were safe from the fierce warriors called the Moors. The rich valleys, the towns and the castles of the south had been conquered by these Moors who had invaded Spain from north Africa. On their swift Arabian horses, armed with lances and their curving swords called scimitars, they rode into battle shouting 'Allah! Allah!' at the tops of their voices. Allah was their god, and they conquered north Africa in his honour. In Spain these Moors settled down. They built fine cities and palaces. By using water wisely they turned barren land into farms. And so Spain was divided between Christians and Moors, and wars constantly raged between the two sides.

One of the Christian kings was Fernando, King of Castile. He was an old man with three sons. One day he called a council meeting of all his nobles to decide how to fight the Moors. To this meeting came Rodrigo de Vivar, seventeen years of age and poor, but already a fine swordsman. At the court he saw a young woman, Jimena. In an instant he knew that he loved Jimena.

But at this same meeting was Jimena's father, the Count of Lozano, a powerful knight. The Count insulted Rodrigo's father, calling him a coward. Rodrigo's father was an old man, and so Rodrigo challenged the Count to fight a duel.

They fought with swords in the courtyard of the Count's castle. Rodrigo's great strength began to tell. Suddenly, he saw Jimena at the edge of the crowd watching the struggle.

'Count!' Rodrigo cried. 'Beg my father's pardon, and we shall end this quarrel.'

'I ask no pardon of cowards,' the Count replied, angrily.

At this fresh insult Rodrigo swung his sword and sliced through the Count's shield and helmet. Jimena cried out in horror as her father fell dead.

The King of Castile ordered Rodrigo to appear before him. Rodrigo expected to be punished.

But instead the King made him kneel and touched his shoulder with a sword.

'You are too good a soldier to die,' he said. 'I make you a knight.' Rodrigo was amazed. But the King had not finished with him.

'You have killed the Count of Lozano. For your punishment you will do battle alone against the Moors.'

Rodrigo rode away into the wild country that lay between the Christian and the Moorish kingdoms. A band of young men joined him, for his fame as a soldier soon spread throughout Spain. His raids on the Moors were full of daring, and the Arabs came to fear and respect him.

One day Rodrigo and his band saw a group of Moorish horsemen protecting several rich merchants on the road to the city of Zaragoza. The knights swooped down, drove off the Arab horsemen and captured a great treasure. Riding one of the mules was a Moorish princess. Tears ran down her cheeks.

'She is to be the bride of the Emir of Zaragoza,' one of the merchants told him. 'She is to be married in a week.'

Rodrigo's men wanted to take the princess with them, to make the Emir pay a huge ransom for her. But Rodrigo remembered how he was separated from Jimena. He would not bring the same misfortune to another.

'Let them go,' he said. 'We shall not spoil a wedding. But tell the Emir that he is a fool to leave such a jewel with so weak a guard.'

At that moment a group of bandits rode up. They wanted to kill the princess and the merchants and divide the treasure between them all. To settle the dispute Rodrigo challenged the bandit leader to a fight. After a great struggle, the bandit leader fell dead. When the merchants reached the city of Zaragoza, they spread the story of how Rodrigo had saved them. From that time onwards he became known by the name that the Moors gave him – *El Cid*, *Campeador* which means 'My Lord, the Champion'. And the Emir, grateful for the return of his bride, became an ally and friend.

El Cid was now the greatest knight in Spain, and King Fernando called him back to Castile to become the Champion, commander-in-chief of the King's armies. He fought for the King in single-handed combats and as a general in command of large armies.

Jimena forgave him and they were married. But when the old King died, his three sons soon

quarrelled among themselves. The eldest son was killed, and the new King of Castile, Alfonso, was jealous of Rodrigo's fame. So El Cid went to live in the country with Jimena, his son and two daughters.

As the years passed, it became clear that Spain still needed El Cid. In North Africa a new leader, Yusuf, took command of the Arab armies. He was a great soldier who dressed simply in a black cloak and who could go for weeks on wild berries and camel's milk. He prepared a fleet of hundreds of ships and sailed to Spain. The news of his landing made men tremble. The cruelty and the bravery of Yusuf's soldiers made everyone fear them.

Alfonso gathered an army and attacked the Moors. But Yusuf baited a trap. He pretended to retreat, and the Christian horsemen galloped in pursuit. They were surrounded and cut to pieces. King Alfonso fled to a castle nearby, badly wounded.

At this point the King called on El Cid to return. So, once again Rodrigo led the armies of Spain against the Moors. He advanced on the great city of Valencia, protected by its castle on the seashore. By this time Yusuf had captured most of southern Spain. He marched towards Valencia. El Cid's army was trapped. On one side was Yusuf's black-robed army, their drums beating steadily, day and night. Between the Christians and the sea lay Valencia, still held by the Moors.

But over the years El Cid had learned cunning. He retreated into the fields, and Yusuf's army followed him. Then he ordered the gates of the canals to be opened. Water poured out, and in the night the Arabs found themselves wallowing in mud and water. Thousands of the Moors believed El Cid to be a wizard with magic powers. Now he had made fields into swamps. The Moors fled, and the city of Valencia surrendered to El Cid. Mounted on his white horse, wearing armour of gold and silver, he entered the city at the head of his troops. On his shoulder was a

shield with a red dragon at its centre. One hand rested on his lance, and the other held the reins of his horse.

'Let there be no killing,' ordered El Cid, 'for these Moors, unlike Yusuf, are our friends.'

All the people came out to cheer, and a golden crown was offered to Rodrigo.

'The King! The King of Valencia!' the crowd shouted.

'I will rule you,' El Cid replied, 'as Governor in the name of King Alfonso.' Although the King had been ungrateful to him, El Cid was loyal.

The wars against the Moors went on and on. Yusuf returned to Valencia and for ten days he hurled his army against the walls of the city. When the enemy grew weary, El Cid led his knights out of the gates of the city. The entire

Moorish army was driven into the sea. Again the Christians were able to breathe, with the Moors fleeing to their own cities.

More years passed. Rodrigo's son grew up, became a knight and was killed in the King's army, fighting against the Moors led by Yusuf's son. Thus the Moors took their revenge on El Cid.

But the long struggle between Rodrigo and Yusuf had not yet ended. For the third time the Moors invaded Spain from north Africa. Again they linked up with the Moorish emirs and advanced on Valencia. El Cid waited until the

Moors had made camp. Then he wheeled up giant catapults that fired boulders upon the tents of the sleeping enemy. The Moors were terrified. The same wizard who had drowned one army now caused boulders to rain on them from the sky! To fight against him was to fight against the Devil! Panic swept through their army, and they fled from the field.

In the pursuit of Yusuf, El Cid's famous white horse stumbled over a tent rope and threw him to the ground. His shoulder was broken and he became unconscious. When he awoke, Jimena was wiping his forehead with a cool cloth.

'Why do you weep?' he asked her, gently. 'For we have won another great victory. Our son has been revenged.'

81

El Cid had often been wounded. But this time the broken bones became infected, and within a few days he died. In Valencia knights and soldiers wept in the streets when they heard the sad news. Who would protect them from the Moors?

'What shall we do, madam?' the people of Valencia asked Jimena. 'The Arabs will return to attack us now that El Cid is dead.'

'If you would honour his memory,' she declared, 'you will defend his city to the last. I for one shall stay here, alone if I have to.'

Within a short time the Moors had indeed returned to Valencia. Alfonso, who had been jealous of Rodrigo when he was alive, now came to the rescue of Jimena. On the hundredth day of the siege of the city King Alfonso arrived with an army. But the huge horde of Yusuf's army still waited patiently outside the walls. Only one man could have saved Valencia, Jimena and the King. But he was dead.

Next morning, at the light of dawn, the Moorish sentries saw the great gates of Valencia swing open. Drums rolled to awaken the army. The horses were brought forward, and sharp scimitars were waved by forty thousand Moors.

Suddenly, a great wail of terror went up from the ranks of the Moorish army. Mounted knights rode out from the city gate. First among them came a white horse with the banners of the Cid on its flanks. Riding on the horse was a knight that they all knew. It could not be – him! Yusuf and his men cried out in horror. It was the Cid himself who led the charge, sitting upright in his saddle, his sword gleaming by his side. Surely the legends were true! El Cid was a demon from the underworld – the Devil himself!

Yusuf's army fled. King Alfonso did not pursue them once the tide of black-cloaked men had thrown away their swords in their flight. His knights surrounded the white horse, its rider still sitting erect, his sightless eyes staring over their heads. It was the body of El Cid, swathed in bandages and strapped to his horse. He had taken the field for the last time and again had won a victory. Jimena, the King and the knights escaped from the city of Valencia and returned to Castile. El Cid was given a hero's burial in a monastery and was later laid to rest in the cathedral.

The Flying Dutchman

The Dutch people have always been afraid of the sea. With storm-driven waves at their doorstep (and sometimes breaking across the threshold and into their front parlour), they have had to fight and conquer the greedy floods that tried to cover their low-lying land. Among the many stories about Dutchmen who have struggled against the power of the sea is the strange tale of Captain Van der Decken.

The Captain was known to be a violent man. The crews of his ships feared him because of his furious temper and great rages. If a ship did not sail fast enough for his liking, he would refuse to feed his crew. If a seaman did not climb the rigging quickly, he was tied to a mast and flogged. On the other hand, he had a brother who was gentle and kind. The brother looked after the family business while the Captain sailed the southern seas, bringing cargoes to their home port in Holland. At the end of one of his voyages Captain Van der Decken returned home to find his brother sad and anxious.

'I have bad news for you,' said his brother.

'What is it, man?' demanded the Captain.

'The last cargo that you brought home had rotted in the hold of the ship,' his brother replied. 'I had to throw it all away. We are ruined, for there is no money to carry on our trade.'

The Captain raged at him. What a fool he had been to trust the business to a simpleton. The brother answered that many Dutch people would no longer trade with them because of the Captain's cruelty to his seamen. At this truthful remark Captain Van der Decken raised his fist and struck his brother, knocking him to the floor. The falling man hit his head against the edge of the iron fireplace and in a moment lay dead at the Captain's feet. He was horrified: his temper had led to many terrible crimes but none as cruel as this.

The Dutch townspeople dragged the Captain before the judges who gave sentence. He was to join his ship and sail away to the south seas, never again to return to Holland.

Sadly, the Captain set sail. At first all went well. He kept to his cabin, brooding on the tragic death of his brother. The crew sailed the ship out of the harbour, across the northern seas and into the great southern ocean.

Off the southern tip of Africa the ship ran into a violent storm which ripped the sails and tore holes in its side. The mate knocked at the Captain's cabin door.

'We must turn the vessel and run for shelter!' he implored. 'The ship cannot last another hour!'

Captain Van der Decken roused himself and came up on deck. The wind howled through the torn sails, a mast lay broken across the deck, and the ship surged on through mountainous seas that reared about them like great sea monsters.

''Tis nothing! A gentle breeze!' the Captain scoffed. 'You are old women, afraid of a wind. Turn the ship into the gale, helmsman, and put your trust in the Devil.'

The crew gasped in alarm. They were all religious men and thought the Captain must be mad to mock God in this foolish manner. The Dutchman ignored them. He stood at the ship's rail,

called for a mug of ale and lit his pipe. Unconcerned, it was as if he stood at the bar of an ale-house in his own home town in Holland.

The crew again begged him to shorten sail and to run for harbour. But the Captain became even more obstinate: as each sail was torn to ribbons, he laughed as if it was a joke and sang songs that mocked God. One brave man seized the ship's wheel and struggled to turn the vessel on a new course towards harbour. The Captain picked him up and threw him overboard.

A flash of lightning and the crack of thunder stunned the crew. The figure of an old man, clad in a long white cloak, appeared on the deck. The seamen fell back, deeply afraid, but the Captain, was quite unconcerned and continued to puff at his pipe.

'You are a cruel man,' said the apparition. 'You would happily take all these poor men with you to your doom.'

'I fear no one,' boasted the Captain. 'Not even a ghost such as you. Begone! If not, your white shirt will soon be stained with blood.'

The old man looked calmly at the Captain. Enraged, Van der Decken pulled a pistol from his belt, took careful aim and fired. The bullet, instead of striking the white-bearded man, pierced the Captain's own hand. The Dutchman stepped forward and raised his clenched fist to club the old man to the deck. But his arm fell paralysed to his side. His rage deepened and he swore at God for all his misery and pain.

The old man spoke again. 'You are cursed, Captain. And there is a punishment for evil men such as you. Henceforward you are condemned to sail the oceans of the world for ever. You will never take shelter in any harbour nor step on any land again.'

The Captain now fell silent.

The ghost went on. 'No crew will ever serve under such a master. You will sail alone. Your hand will be always at the ship's wheel, and if your eyes close, the point of a sword will awaken you.'

'It is a terrible punishment,' the Captain said, very quietly.

'The roll-call of your doom is not complete,' the old man continued. 'Wherever you sail, a storm will follow you. Men will therefore say, "Beware! Here comes The Flying Dutchman. Avoid him, or your ship will be wrecked."'

'And will there be no end to this voyage?' asked the Captain.

'You must learn to love your fellow men,' the ghost told him. 'You will sail the oceans for hundreds of years. It is possible that in time you may find a woman who will be your wife and will travel with you across the seas. If she can teach you kindness and compassion, you may be saved. There are good women in the world. But it will be a long search to find such a wife.'

The old man vanished. Then the crew disappeared. The Dutchman was left alone on board

his ship. He cursed and swore against God, the ghost and all mankind. And so a great storm came up to buffet and pursue him, and he began his long, endless voyage.

Since that day the Flying Dutchman has sailed at the very centre of many storms. He has been blamed for many shipwrecks, for driving unfortunate seamen on to dangerous rocks and into shoals. His ship has changed colour and shape. It was often seen as a tall sailing ship with black sails, sometimes a slim and swift yacht, sometimes a heavy, ugly vessel like a Dutch barge. Wherever it was seen, it brought disaster.

And what of a wife for the Flying Dutchman? Did he one day pick up a victim from one of the shipwrecks? Did a woman swim out to his yacht as it cruised along a coast? The Flying Dutchman may still be crossing the oceans of the world, still searching for a wife, or he may have met a good woman who has taught him to love mankind, and it is possible that after hundreds of years the phantom ship has reached its last harbour.

Leif Ericsson and the Voyage to Vine-land

Over a thousand years ago a fleet of twenty-five ships set sail from the shores of Iceland. The ships were small, light, with a single square sail to catch the wind. On board were men, women and children, dressed in skins and furs. In the ships' holds were cattle and sheep, horses and pigs, bales of hay for the animals, dried fish, dried meat, cheese and butter, tools, hunting weapons and many other things that they needed for a new life.

In the prow of the leading ship stood Erik the Red. The Viking leader had persuaded his people to leave the shores of Iceland and seek new lands to the west of the island.

'It will be a difficult voyage,' Erik told his people. 'There will be storms, and mountains of ice floating in the sea, and all manner of dangers.'

Erik spoke truthfully, for strong winds and icebergs sank nine of the frail ships before they sailed into the shelter of a fjord. The coast looked familiar, for Erik had been born in Norway.

'Look!' cried one of the Vikings.

Along the side of the fjord, below the snow and ice of the mountains, were green slopes where grass grew freely.

'Let us call our new land ''Greenland'' to mark our safe arrival,' said Erik. 'Bjarne, our kinsman, who has sailed in these seas, told us that there were pastures for our sheep beyond the mountains of ice. Bjarne spoke truly.'

The Vikings went ashore and set up tents. They began the work of cutting timber to build the long wooden houses in which they lived. Soon, a town of the long-houses, protected from the wind by the shelter of the valley, grew up along the shore of the fjord.

Years passed: the settlers grew corn in the short summers, hunted reindeer and whales and sheltered from the icy winds and heavy winter snow in their snug long-houses. As a boy, one of Erik's sons, Leif, loved to sail up and down the fjords. As he grew older, he cast his eyes more and more towards the setting sun in the west, remembering stories told around the evening fires of strange lands that lay over the horizon. As the months passed and Leif looked longingly across the grey sea to where it met the grey sky, the idea of a voyage to explore this world grew more and more powerful in his mind.

Leif told his father of his ambition. Erik thought long and hard.

'The settlement is safe now,' he said. 'Though I am an old man, the sea still calls me. But you are young and strong. We shall both sail to the strange land. But you will be the leader, and I will be one of your crew.'

The ship they built was long and narrow. Their shields were hung out over the side, for every cranny of space was filled with clothing, tools and dried meat. The ship was so shallow that when it was loaded the Vikings could touch the sea with their hands as they sat at the oars. Leif loved the way the light vessel skimmed over the waves, the square sail straining against the wind. There was no shelter, no cabin for the crew. When the gales blew and icy rain fell, the men had to burrow more deeply into their fur-lined cloaks.

Let the Vikings sail again! With a blast on the horns echoing around the fjords of Greenland, the Viking ship set sail, with the whole settlement lining the shore to wave goodbye. Leif left the land behind within a day and steered by the sun. He could tell from its position how far north or south they were from Greenland. But there were many days without the sun, when heavy grey clouds obscured the sky. Sometimes mists covered the sea, and huge floating mountains of ice suddenly appeared before them.

After many days at sea, the crew began to mutter amongst themselves, fearing that they were lost and would never again see their homelands. Then, out of the mist, they saw the snowy peak of a distant mountain. As the longship sailed close to the shore, Leif looked for the sight of green grass and trees, but nothing met his gaze but a wasteland of snow and rocks.

'We must go inland,' Erik suggested.

Leif shouted an order to cast the anchor, and a rowboat soon took them to the shores of the new land. The Vikings searched the shores of the fjord, but all that grew there were a few stunted trees and the moss that reindeer ate. They crossed wide glaciers and slipped and cut themselves on jagged rocks. It took them a full day to climb the mountain. From its peak the Vikings gazed with dismay at a land that seemed to be made entirely of rock, with a hundred lakes glistening under the grey, unfriendly sky.

'Return to the ship,' Leif ordered his men. 'This is a terrible place. Let us name it "Helluland" – the land of stone.'

They sailed on, south again, and landed at several places on the coast. At last they arrived

at a country covered with leafy woodlands. The Vikings dropped anchor and went ashore. They grasped their short swords and held their iron-rimmed shields in front of them, fearing an attack. But the only wild things they saw were small animals and birds that took fright and scampered away into the bushes.

Leif liked the new land. He took off his helmet and waved it in a sign.

'This place shall be called Mark-land, the land of woods,' he declared.

They carried on again, running before a wind. The sun grew warmer, and they noticed many different fish in the sea. They reached a large island and sailed around it, and then came to a wide river. All this was unknown land, for none of the story-tellers, the writers of the sagas, had told about it. By this time Leif knew that winter was approaching and he did not dare to risk a return voyage to Greenland in this season.

He ordered the crew to go ashore. The ship was dragged up on a beach, and again the axes swung to fell trees for winter shelter. As the days passed, the Vikings were amazed to find that frost did not cover the ground or make it as hard as iron, as in Greenland. The rivers were full of fat salmon, bigger than anything they had seen before.

Among the Vikings was a man called Tyrker who had travelled to many lands. It was said that he came from Turkey, and this explained his name. He often went off hunting alone and returned with an animal for their feasts. One day it was dark when he returned.

'Why are you out so late?' Leif asked him. 'There is great danger in going alone into the woods.'

The warrior opened the palm of his hand to show six smooth round dark-skinned fruits. Leif peered at them.

'What is it?' he asked. 'Is it a poison that makes you ill?'

'When I was a young man,' replied Tyrker, 'I went on many voyages and raids. In some of the southern lands the people grow these fruits. The plant is called the vine, and the fruits grapes.'

Leif ate the grapes and marvelled at their sweetness. Next day he sent men with Tyrker to collect grapes and bring them to the camp. They gathered up the fruit and added it to the evening feast. Leif was pleased with the find.

'We shall name this fair country Vine-land,' he told the men, and they sang Viking songs to celebrate old victories and the conquest of this new, rich land.

On the next day the warriors thought they saw dark men watching them from the forest, but they seemed to melt away into the bushes, to vanish from sight. When spring came, they gathered more of the fruit, loaded their ship and set sail. They were eager to see their families again in far-off Greenland. Leif watched the sun and followed a course that within a few weeks brought him and the ship to the cold mountains of Greenland. The whole of the township came down to the beach to welcome them. Leif hugged his wife Gudrid and promised to stay at home. But the call of the sea was in his blood, and in the next year the crew, led by Leif Ericsson, went roving the seas of the north again.

Leif had a young brother, Thorvald, who wanted to share in the glory. He took command of the next expedition to Vine-land. The Vikings followed Leif's advice and found the countries of Helluland and Mark-land. They went south until they saw the vines and grapes.

'This is a beautiful place,' declared Thorvald, 'where I would be glad to make my home.'

When they returned to their ship, a look-out blew an alarm on his horn. Around the headland came a war-party of natives in eight canoes. They were the first men that the Vikings had seen in this new land.

With swords and axes raised high, the Vikings waited for the attack.

'Set your war-shields over the side,' shouted Thorvald. 'Defend the ship, for if we lose it we shall never see our homes again.'

The savages came in close, firing arrows from short bows. The Vikings were helpless for they could not strike at the natives with their swords. The sail was raised, and the ship was rammed into the canoes. At this the savages turned and fled.

'Is any man wounded?' Thorvald called out.

No one answered. Thorvald raised his arm. Red blood poured in a stream from an arrow deep in his side.

'I have a death-wound,' he said. 'An arrow flew under my shield. Carry me to that headland and bury me there.'

His crew, full of sadness, did as he wished. Thorvald was the only Viking to remain in Vineland. The rest of the crew stayed until winter passed and then, with the ship packed with grapes and other wild fruit, they returned to Greenland.

In the long winters of Greenland the explorers told their stories around the leaping fires of the long-houses. These stories were written down and became the 'sagas', the tales of the Northmen. And where were these lands of woods and vines, far across the ocean, south of Greenland? Hundreds of years before the explorers of Spain, Portugal and England 'discovered' the New World, the Vikings perhaps sailed down the coast of America, fought the native savages of that country and left one of their leaders, Thorvald, buried there. Was the beautiful rich Vineland found by Leif Ericsson and his brother Thorvald the same country that became known as America? What do you think?

Sitting Bull

Among the Hunkpapa tribe, part of the great Sioux nation, lived a boy who had killed his first buffalo when he was ten and now, four years later, was ready to become a warrior. The boy's father, Jumping Bull, was leader of the tribe, and as the boy watched him and other warriors preparing a war-party, he wished he could go with them. The enemies of the Hunkpapa were the Crow tribe, fearless fighters who raided the hunting grounds sacred to the Sioux.

The painted warriors mounted their horses and rode off across the prairie. When they were out of sight, the boy jumped on his pony and trailed them to a creek where the Hunkpapa met up with other Sioux tribesmen. An alert scout spotted the boy in the cover of the trees and he was brought before his father, Jumping Bull.

'What are you doing here, boy?' his father asked, grimly.

'I am going to hunt the Crow too,' the boy replied.

The other braves laughed and made jokes about children trying to be men. No boy of fourteen had ridden with the warriors. Jumping Bull with a raised hand stopped the chatter.

'My son will ride with us,' he said.

The other Indians shrugged and turned their backs. The boy would die. Crow warriors had no mercy.

For days they hunted across the Great Plains until they came to the bank of a wide river. A scout was sent to the top of a hill while the tribesmen started their cooking fires. The scout soon raced back, shouting that a Crow war-party was approaching.

The boy painted himself for battle. His grey horse was streaked with red paint. He himself was painted yellow from head to toe. He wore only a waist-cloth, a string of beads and his moccasins. The Sioux, like other Indian tribes, attacked in the way they always used. They rode straight at the enemy, yelling loudly to frighten them into running. No one gave orders: it was known that you killed or were killed. The Crow saw that they had ridden into a trap and wheeled their horses about to run for cover. The Hunk-papa and Sioux raced after them, howling with rage. The boy was light; his horse was fast; and soon he was in the lead, armed only with a stick. He caught up with a Crow warrior just as the brave was drawing his bow. The boy rode in close and lashed the Crow's arm with the stick, spoiling his aim. Jumping Bull was only a step or two behind: he swooped in for the kill. A quick strike with his tomahawk, and the enemy tribesman fell from his horse to lie dead in the dust of the plain. The running battle was soon over. At the end of it the Sioux had six scalps, horses and weapons. The victors rode home in good humour.

The boy, although he had not killed anyone, was the hero. His horse was painted black from the tip of its head to its hooves in honour of the battle. Black was the colour of victory in the Sioux tribe.

'My son went to war with the enemies of our people,' Jumping Bull told the village elders. 'I proclaim him to be a warrior and I give him a new name. Everyone hear this! This boy, my son, will be known as Sitting Bull.'

This name, Sitting Bull, was to become well known and feared by both the Indian tribes on the Great Plains and by the white men who came to conquer the territory of the braves. Eventually he became the war chief of all the Sioux tribes and led them against the armies of the white men.

But before he became a chief Sitting Bull had to prove himself as a warrior. Among all the tribes the Crow continued to be their bitterest enemies. As Sitting Bull grew up to take his place in the ranks of the Warrior Society, he knew that

one day the Crow would seek revenge for their many defeats.

The Hunkpapa tribe did not stay for long in one place. Instead, they followed the buffalo as they wandered across the Great Plains. One day the tribe packed all their possessions on their horses and mules and set off. Foolishly, no scouts were posted, and suddenly from the shadow of some trees fifty painted Crow warriors appeared. The women and children scattered in panic, running here and there to seek shelter from the flying arrows. Even the warriors were confused and dashed around, shouting at each other. The Crow struck at the head of the column and killed two boys who were leading the mules. Jumping Bull, yelling orders, collected his warriors and rode off to fight the attackers. A running battle developed in the long grass of the prairie. Jumping Bull was separated from the others in the fight. On the banks of a creek a Crow brave jumped off his horse and signalled to the chief to fight on foot – and to the death. The Crow had a musket; all Jumping Bull had was his hunting knife. As the Sioux warrior ran towards his enemy, the Crow raised his gun and fired. The bullet hit Jumping Bull in the shoulder, but the chief kept on running. He hurled himself at the brave, and both men fell to the ground, grappling with their knives.

Wounded by the bullet, Jumping Bull's strength ebbed away, and the Crow was able to stab him again and again in the chest. Sitting Bull arrived just in time to see the Crow rising from his father's corpse. He set off in hot pursuit: nothing else mattered except to avenge the death of Jumping Bull. For hours he trailed the Crow across the prairie and through the woods. Slowly his horse overhauled his enemy until he was only the length of a lance away. With a single wild cry, he hurled his lance and brought the Crow crashing to the ground. Sitting Bull leaped from his horse and thrust his knife deep into the brave.

After he rejoined the Sioux column, Sitting Bull was so angry that he led the warriors in an attack on the Crow camp. They rode for thirty miles, chasing and harrying their enemies. For every Sioux killed they knifed three Crow, including women and children. Even young babies were put to death.

As the years passed, Sitting Bull rose to become chief of the Hunkpapa tribe and in this time he showed no mercy to any of the other tribes except other Sioux. One day, deep in the forest, they came across another Crow tribe encamped by the ice-covered river Missouri. The Hunkpapa caught them in their tepees, and few escaped. Men, women and children were all hunted down and killed. All Indian tribes knew that you must never leave any child alive – one day, after he had grown up, he would return to avenge the death of his family.

Of the enemy only one boy of about eleven remained alive. He stood patiently beside the bodies of his brothers, sisters, father and mother. He would fight with his knife until he was killed. One by one the Hunkpapa braves rode towards him and touched him with their sticks. This was a sign of conquest and of death.

When they had all touched the boy, a warrior would ride in to strike him down with a tomahawk. This is how warriors always acted towards their enemies. Sitting Bull walked up to the boy. His own father had been killed by the Crow; his mother had died of disease; he had no brothers or sisters; no wife and no children.

Suddenly he shouted: 'Do not kill this boy! He is too brave to die!'

'He is of an enemy tribe,' one chief pointed out. 'When he is a man, he will kill our people.'

'I have no brothers,' pleaded Sitting Bull. 'Let him stay with me and become my brother.'

In the end the other chiefs decided that the elders of all the Sioux tribes must decide. So Sitting Bull pulled the boy on to his horse and rode back to the village. He painted the lad in Sioux colours, gave him new clothes and made him ride and walk beside him. Then he gave the boy a new name – Jumping Bull, the name of his own father. All the elders and warriors then knew that if they ruled that the boy should die they would have to fight Sitting Bull.

At the council of elders Sitting Bull spoke up. 'I have made him my brother,' he said, simply. 'If you kill him, you will have to fight and kill me.'

The elders consented, and in the years to come the adoption of the Crow boy was talked about as one of Sitting Bull's greatest achievements. No Indian tribe had ever allowed a stranger to join them. But the young Jumping Bull was loyal to the Sioux. In time he became one of the greatest hunters and warriors in the tribe.

Within a few years the Sioux turned away from their old enemies to deal with the white men who crossed the great rivers and settled on the Indians' ancient hunting grounds. To guard the farmers and settlers the US cavalry built forts and patrolled the new roads. More and more, Sitting Bull had to fight the cavalry patrols to protect the Sioux lands.

At first Sitting Bull thought that the white men could be driven away. They were loaded down with equipment and in battle they all bunched together like women. But there were so many of them. Their patrols had many men and soon outnumbered the Sioux by ten to one.

When Sitting Bull was thirty-five years old, he was elected chief of chiefs of the Sioux nation and he led them to many victories. Perhaps his greatest triumph of all was in the long war against the white men. One day General Custer rode into the valley of the Little Big Horn with an army of blue-coated cavalrymen. Unknown to the General, a great army of Sioux led by Sitting Bull had made camp in the nearby hills.

General Custer made the mistake of riding deep into Indian territory, shooting and killing. He was surrounded by the warriors who, after years of defeat by the horse-soldiers, knew that they had a great victory in their grasp. Wave after wave of painted braves rode against the thinning circle of cavalrymen, until in less than an hour every white soldier, including General Custer, lay dead. This was the last great battle between the Sioux and the soldiers from the East. It ended in a victory for the warriors. But as Sitting Bull sat by the camp-fire with the victory dances going on around him, he stared at the flames.

'I think,' he told his adopted brother, 'we must be ready for a time of great trouble.'

And, indeed, the blue-coated cavalry soldiers were to return, angry and determined. Many other battles were fought before the Indian tribes were finally overwhelmed, but to the end the legend of Sitting Bull remained to inspire the tribes as they sat around their camp-fires and told the stories of their grandfathers in the days before the white men came.

GEORGETOWN PEABODY LIBRARY
GEORGETOWN, MASS.